UTE!

by the author of CARNAL ORGY

CON SELLERS

WILDSIDE PRESS

THE "BRUTE" MEETS BRUTE

The shriek came keening up the hatchway, full of pain and hate. A woman in agony, the sound torn from the throat of his lover!

He threw himself at the sliver of yellow light, tore at the hatch cover and hurled it into the night. Brad leaped feet first into the cabin below.

Gleaming nakedly and stretched painfully taut like an "X" of lovely flesh, she hung between iron ringbolts. There was a fleck of blood on each of her beautiful breasts. A man caught up in the insane folds of a nightmare, Brad started for her.

Getty stepped out from behind the bar and aimed a .38 at Brad's middle. There was a sickly shine of sweat on his jowls.

Brad tensed. "Hit me right, Getty—stop me with the first one, or I'll stick that gun down your throat . . ."

A raging blur, Brad leaped toward Getty. The .38 slammed, seared flame and slug—

BR

CHAPTER I

The New Opal Hotel wasn't new any longer, but it was still shiny with a cheap, touched-up glitter. It was smaller than he remembered, too; at least from the outside.

Brad Saxon stood on the narrow sidewalk, oblivious to the traffic clangor behind him, to the hurrying, chattering throng that swirled around him. Nine years and six thousand miles of ocean rolled back; he was a young trooper again, a little drunk, a little eager for his first taste of the vaunted Japanese women. Nine years? It couldn't be.

Brad shook himself, and knew that it had been. He didn't know what the hell he was waiting for. Music throbbed from behind the New Opal's door, backgrounded by the rattle of glasses and throaty laughter. That much hadn't changed.

But she might not be there, and that's what was keeping him standing outside, keeping him afraid to go in. He shifted weight from his trick leg, barely conscious of the awed glances of passing Japanese. Brad was used to being stared at. He wasn't pretty, by a damned sight. Thrusting helmets and grinding shoulder pads and sly elbows hadn't improved on a face that wasn't much to start with; the cleat scar twisting one corner of his mouth made him look particularly satanic. Except the devil never had such a repeatedly broken nose. And Brad was even bigger in this land of little men—towering over the slim people. Bulking wide and thick like one of their stone demons.

Inside, a girl laughed high and tinkly. Brad swallowed hard. It sounded like Sueko, but so had all the women he'd heard since the plane landed. And they all had something of her in them, some tilt of their bluesheen heads, some innate grace in their tripping walks. Maybe he had come back to Japan to seek only an image.

Brad shook his head again. No; Sueko was the only real thing he'd known. Time couldn't build a fantasy around her, couldn't brighten the aura she already had.

"Hey Joe."

Brad looked down at the tug on his sleeve, at the kid grinning old and wise up at him.

"You want girl, Joe?"

"No," Brad lied, glad for this outward impetus that shoved him at the doorway of the New Opal Hotel.

He had to stoop, and angle the width of his shoulders to pass through, and the place even smelled the same—eddying cigaret smoke, beersweet odors, the drifting scents of a dozen perfumes.

The girl came gliding from neon shadows, sway-hipping in a tight red gown that plunged low between the modeled cones of arching breasts. Midnight hair cascaded richly over creamed ivory shoulders; ripe lips parted in a damp smile; the direct almond eyes—and the woman smell of her touched with sandalwood and spices.

But it wasn't Sueko.

"Hello," the girl said, and put a pale butterfly hand against his arm.

B-girl; hustler, hostess—and she didn't act like one; none of them did. Not like the c'mon-gimmie-a-drink wenches in San Francisco and New Orleans; not like the greedy broads in a hundred other Stateside towns. Gentle; unhurried; the here-for-your-desire girls of the Orient.

6

"Hello," Brad said, lifting his eyes then to search the shadowed corners of the bar. One girl dealing herself a hand of solitaire at a tiny table, waiting for the evening rush to begin. Another sorting records at a portable phonograph, a young GI with his arm about her trim waist. The lacquered face of the madam behind the bar, waiting. No one else. But it was early; maybe Sueko hadn't come down yet.

Brad glanced down at the girl again. "Mind sitting at the bar? I'd like to talk to you."

He saw the hidden wariness, the balanced intentness go out of her. He could almost sense the working of her mind, the relief that this big one wasn't drunk and brutal, even if he was ugly. Brad smiled at her, the old cleat mark twisting his mouth high on one side. The adage about treating a prostitute like a lady never held truer than in Japan, where most of the "business girls" could give cards and spades to some of the "ladies" Brad knew in the States and still come out ahead.

He cupped the girl's elbow, helped her lift to sit on the stool. Her smile turned genuine. The madam waited, expressionless. Brad lifted a mangled eyebrow at the girl. "Port wine still the drink?"

She blinked sloe eyes, nodded slowly. "If—you wish."

Port wine, the B-drink of the Orient, Asiatic substitute for the "champagne" other girls across the sea were conning out of visiting firemen. It came in a champagne glass, all right—a pale purple squirt of wine over a double handful of crushed ice.

"*O-sake* for me," Brad said. "Hot," and marked himself as a man who'd been some time in the Far East.

The girl's words were accented, but showed an effort to break away from typical GI English; her voice had a lilt to it. Like Sueko's. "My name Marie," she said.

7

"Or Mariko," Brad said, "or maybe Machiko. Which is it?"

She dimpled. "Machiko, but GIs don't say that. Marie easier."

"Machiko is prettier; do you mind if I use it?"

Machiko covered momentary embarrassment with a sip at her wine. "No."

Brad's sake came in its little bowl of hot water. The small graceful bottle seemed lost in his big hand. He asked the question. "Is—Sueko still here?"

Prettily, she frowned. "Sueko?"

"Kamiya," Brad said, hurrying, "Kamiya Sueko. She works here."

Did she, after nine years? Did she still make the unconscious motion of drawing her hands up into the flowing sleeves of the *yukata*, turning the prosaic sleeping kimono into the shape of a hovering butterfly? Did she—

"Sueko," he repeated, his hand clenching the smoothness of her arm. "You know Kamiya Sueko, don't you?"

Machiko bit her lips. "P-please—"

Brad took his hand away. "I'm sorry; I didn't mean to hurt you."

The girl moistened her mouth, dark eyes flicking beyond him. She started to say something.

"No Sueko here," the madam said, at his elbow. "You got wrong hotel."

Brad explained. It had been a long time ago, but this was the place. He remembered the rooms across the courtyard—one of them, anyway. He could describe that one to the last detail. Painted face showing nothing, the madam shrugged.

"Many girls," she said. "All time come, go. No Sueko here now."

Machiko's eyes fell when the madam stared at her.

"Okay," Brad said. "I'll find her somewhere."

When the madam drifted away, Brad told Machiko about the girl he was seeking. It had been Spring

8

then; prophetically, it was Spring now, the startlingly fresh green bursting forth; the hint of cherry blossoms in clear air. And a younger Brad Saxon like the season's early colt, bouncing awkwardly, without direction.

A bitter young man, certainly. With the stark coldness of black mountains too recently on him; with the icy hate of dirty little men and bright blood spilled on the alien snows of Korea.

Brad's face hadn't been so scarred then, but it was stamped with agonies and a deep-smouldering rage, an impotent, bottled-up anger that threatened to boil out and destroy all near it. Chronologically, he was young, but even the very young age swiftly in combat. At least, the survivors do.

And prisoners turn old even faster. Those that are left after death marches through the stained snow; those who remain after beatings and starvation and torture. When these things happen, men are ancient before their time, brittle and inwardly corroded by their hates.

Nine years after, and who remembered the shattered village of Kunu-ri? You found the name only in yellowed files of newspapers—and engraved on the souls of men who had bled there. Kunu-ri—and the remnants of the Indianhead Division staggering out of the valley, leaving all its artillery, most of its trucks and tanks behind it. Leaving 4,464 dead and missing.

Only all of them weren't dead—yet. A thousand or so were left to be herded into stinking boxcars, to be prodded by bayonets and hammered with gun butts; to be left with ice films glazing blind eyes. Brad Saxon wouldn't die like that. And he wouldn't die in the horror of prison camps to the North.

They thought he was dead when the grimy men in padded uniforms marched his group off to one side of the railroad tracks and opened fire with their burp guns. And he would have been, except for the blood

9

smeared on his face—sticky, hot blood seeping from the fresh corpse beside him.

He didn't remember how long he lay in the trampled snow, stiff, listening to the short bursts of gunfire taking care of the wounded, to the singsong words and sadistic laughter of the slant-eyed animals who had the guns. An eternity crept by before they left, and another eon before Brad dared to lift himself from the heap of dead men. And it wasn't over yet. There was a hundred miles of commie-infested mountains between him and the shocked and reeling outfit. Too far for a Caucasian in an Oriental country.

That's what the books said, anyway. But Brad Saxon had men to kill, so he had to get back. Through frozen gullies, shadow-like over the rocks, a flat snake passing the sheeted ponds of rice paddies, he worked his way South. At Pakc'hon, he strangled a farmer greedy for the reward the Reds were offering for GIs. In Sinanju, he burned another in his ratnest shack. The flames drew guards off the road.

Hollow-eyed, staggering at times, Brad ran and slunk and stole his way toward the UN lines. And he made the hundred miles—only to find there was another hundred to go. Grinding dry rice between aching teeth, choking down odorous *kimchi* dug from buried crocks, Brad went on. He avoided sentries when he could. When he couldn't, he killed them— with his hands, with a broken bayonet, with a loop made from his belt, and later, with accurate bursts from a Russian submachine gun.

The names of towns he'd never forget—Pyongyang, Sariwon, Kaesong, all of them seen only as blurs from a mountaintop, seen only as deadly shadows lurking in a breathheld night. Days fading into hungry weeks, into months. Then the capitol city of Seoul, gripped by victorious Chinese, a ghost city wailing lonely in frozen darkness. Across the numbing waters of the Han, crawling spent and beaten over the shell-pocked highway that led into Yongdongpo.

They were there—the spat! of an M-1, the belated challenge of a wary outpost guard. Brad Saxon was home, but he had more battles ahead. They tried to fly him out to Japan, but he crawled out of the tent hospital and hid until the plane was gone. He wolfed food, and shocked nurses and doctors by his determined calisthenics. It was vital that he get his body back into condition. There were beasts to kill, and Brad needed to kill them.

Technically, he was AWOL when he led a squad of yelling riflemen against a guerilla band—and led the merciless slaughter of them all. On the books, Brad was still a patient in the evacuation hospital when he was a platoon sergeant around whom a legend was building—a legend of revenge and death.

The Chinese stopped his war near Inje, with a bullet through the big tendons back of his left knee. This time, the medics got him aboard a plane, and he fumed helplessly in Tokyo Army Hospital, planning his escape back to Korea as soon as his wound healed. It didn't work out that way.

They gave him a pass into the city, and Brad limped along the strange streets, eager for the taste and feel of a woman. Just any woman wouldn't do; she had to be something special, someone softly feminine and giving and beautiful.

He wandered through the Kyobashi area, drinking in sounds and sights so different from Korea—different, and yet somehow familiarly the same. He looked for the girl, and didn't find her in the glittering Shinbashi bars. On a side street, in the New Opal Hotel, he found her. He found Sueko.

A soft hand closed on his arm, and Brad Saxon jumped.

"You don't like me?"

A sameness in the tilt of oblique cheekbones, a sameness around a rosebud mouth. Brad came back to now, to the girl who wasn't Sueko, but Machiko.

11

He drained the bottle of *sake*, cooled now by the time he'd just spent in the past.

"Sure I like you," he said. "I'm sorry. I guess I was dreaming."

Machiko leaned toward him. The low swoop of her evening gown widened, exposing the dusky cleft between her breasts. She smelled clean, exciting.

"The other girl?"

Brad lifted two fingers at the hovering madam. "Yes. I came back to find her—and I will. Maybe not tonight; maybe next week, next month, but I'll find her."

Machiko kept her face lowered until the woman behind the bar served their drinks and moved away. Then she looked up. "I—hope so."

She smiled at him through a rosy glow, over a parade of *sake* bottles that marched into his big hand. The night rush was on at the New Opal, a pair of soldiers drifting in to look over the merchandise, three more regulars greeted by delighted cries from the girls; the madam joined now by a jacketed bartender. The record player thundered; feet shuffled on the worn floor.

Machiko was sweet; she was sympathetic, and she looked very much like another girl he had once known. Right here in this place. Across the miniature courtyard and down a squeaky hall to a certain room. Suddenly, Brad had to see that room again. He lurched erect with Machiko pattering anxiously beside him. Mumbling apologies, he shouldered across the dance floor. Men frowned at him, but when his size and bulk registered with them, they moved out of his way.

There was no light behind the sliding panels of the remembered door. Brad swayed before it, staring at its blankness.

"This room?" Machiko asked, and when he nodded, she kneeled to remove his shoes.

The imitation Stateside bed was in its usual corner;

the box dresser bare of the statue of Ho-Teh, fat, grinning god of health. It was cold.

"Oh hell," Brad said, realizing that he was drunk, that the waiting and hoping were making him maudlin. "Oh hell," he said again.

The door slid shut behind him. A dim bulb showed him the bones of the room, the unrumpled bed, the withered cherry branch with its tinseled good luck charms hanging dusty from an exposed rafter. It was all wrong. It shouldn't be dim. It ought to be lighted with the glowing beauty of a tiny, modeled girl who tucked her little hands into the sleeves of her *yukata* and looked like a lovely butterfly.

With a delicate motion, Machiko moved in front of him, lifted her hands in an utterly feminine gesture and fluffed out her hair. Dark, searching eyes; dew on the petals of a morning flower; sandalwood and spice, and the urgent thrusting of desire making his belly taut and his loins rigid.

Alien girl, waiting to be sampled, to be tasted and felt; mystery woman, priestess of love cults, of bronze gongs soft in Spring twilight, of silks and satins and perfumed flesh. Fragile girl, so warm and small against the vastness of his body, her slippered feet dangling above the floor.

She held the flavor of warm winds over richly blooming fields, tasting of downy blossoms and far valleys. She was sweetly trembling in his arms, thick hair swirling as he let her go to wriggle out of her dress and bolt the door. She was entrancing hillocks and desirable vales, a flowing together of smooth-warm legs and softflare hips, a clasping, surrendering rocking of thighs and breasts, blending, enveloping. Gladly, he sought to lose himself in her.

And for the moment, she was even tinier, an elfin perfection that clung and spread, and loved in mad-wild passion and an intriguing, gentle tenderness.

He whispered it into the musky sheen of her hair: "Sueko—Sueko—"

13

She didn't stiffen and roll away. If she was hurt, the girl didn't show her pain. Instead, Machiko held him closer, substituting herself for the girl this huge, gentle man dreamed of, wishing in spite of herself that she was actually the one he sought. It would be nice to be so loved.

Brad Saxon sighed back from the girl at last, drained of hasty desire, relaxing in the heady aura of womanhood and the insidious glow of the liquor within him. He was a little puzzled at the way she clung so fervently to him—as if she would never see him again. And he remembered the watchful caution of the hardfaced madam in the bar.

CHAPTER II

From the Classified rooms of the Mainichi newspaper, Brad rode the hurtling little *"kamikaze"* taxi back to his hotel. The Nomura wasn't far from the fabulous Rocker Four Club, most luxurious setup in the world for Army NCOs. It was semi-deserted in the daytime, and passing it, Brad felt a momentary twinge of something indefinable.

Regret? he wondered. No. A sense of being on the outside, perhaps; of not belonging any more. The herd instinct normally strong in man, but stronger yet in the Service. Brad Saxon wasn't sorry he wasn't in uniform any more. The Army was for fighting wars; when there were no more wars, he could see little reason for its existence.

Of course, a standing army was necessary, but that kind of life irked Brad. Spit and polish and the boredom of repeated training; and, he told himself, he mustn't forget the brass-plated and self-appointed gods. A little of them was more than enough. Sure, there were good men in command, even great ones. But there were also the free riders, the desk-and-briefcase politicians who never earned the right to be called soldiers.

Brad crawled out of the cab after it shrieked to a sliding stop outside the Nomura, and paid the gold-toothed hackie. Adding a fat tip, he said: "Here, sport —buy yourself a shrine. You keep driving that way, and you're going to need it."

The driver shrugged fatalistically and roared the

taxi into traffic as Brad turned away and moved through the lobby. The desk clerk bowed slightly when he passed by and into the elevator. Brad grinned to himself. Tokyo—city of no questions asked, as long as you could pay your way. And the big display ad he'd just ordered in the Mainichi should pay its way, too. For the hundred-dollar reward he'd offered, half the city ought to be trying to find Sueko.

At the third floor, Brad turned down the carpeted hall and into his room. There was another lead he could follow himself, the dog-eared, carefully protected letter from Sueko—the last one. Seven years ago, but it had a return address, and not the New Opal Hotel. Her home, perhaps. She'd mentioned a family.

In the shower, Brad let the cool water flow over him, and thought for the hundredth time that his trip might not pay off. Sueko could be dead; she might be married to some GI, living respectably in the States. Brad stepped out and towelled himself. But he had to try. The years away from her had taught him one thing—that all other women stood in her shadow. He had to find her and take her back with him.

Brad plugged in the razor and massaged it over his stubble. Some guys he knew would think he'd flipped; they'd think any man who wanted to marry a prostitute was out of his head. During the past nine years Sueko had probably slept with a thousand men.

But Brad Saxon had been the first. And if he hadn't been such a damned fool, he'd have been the only one. He grimaced at his battered face in the mirror. Well, even damned fools may get another chance, if they're lucky. He wouldn't louse up this opportunity. All the men between didn't matter. Nothing did—except the vital, driving fact that he must hold Sueko in his arms again, permanently.

He took his big, hairy body into the bedroom and began fitting it into a tailored sharkskin suit. Maybe

16

he'd honeymoon in Hong Kong with Sueko, if she liked the idea. They could stock up on good clothes there. Hell, he'd buy her the moon, if she wanted it.

And he could almost afford it. He'd never have to count the bruises again, never have to limp out on the field with the bad knee taped tight, hoping it would hold out through the game. Let the other clowns bang their heads together for the paychecks. Brad Saxon had his.

School had seemed so damned important. The old man had pushed a little, too, wanting Brad to follow him into the State Department. Still, he couldn't blame school—nor the old man—for leaving Sueko as he had. Sure, the Army had a lot to do with it, hustling him back for discharge, tying up marriage applications in red tape. But Brad could have come back as a civilian. He should have come back.

Brad knotted his tie, ran a brush over cropped hair. Maybe he should blame the bid from the Forty-Niners, too. Only you don't blame a job that brought you in almost thirty thousand per. It wasn't bad pay for a big slob who enjoyed banging other big slobs around. A little rough on the hide, perhaps, but tackles weren't supposed to be glamor boys. That was left to the backfield.

He grinned at himself. Some of the old gang were still on the sports pages, still dragging themselves off the field every Sunday. Through the old man's needling and advice, Brad had invested his paychecks in solid payoff stocks, a little finagling here, a little quick selling there. Now he was fat. Now he could afford to run around the world, looking for a certain girl.

If he could find her.

There was a discreet knock on the door. "Yeah?" Brad said.

The man was small and shabby, with rimless spectacles and a jerky manner of bowing. "I'm Mr. Hara. May I come in?"

Brad shrugged. "I've only got a minute. I'm going

17

out." Whatever the guy was selling, Brad didn't want any.

Hara smiled diffidently. "So. To search for Miss Kamiya?"

Brad stared at the little man. "Come in and shut the door. What do you know about her?"

Then he wondered *how* this man knew. The ad wouldn't be in the paper until tomorrow. The New Opal? The girl there? Machiko had seemed to know something, but she'd been afraid to say anything. The omnipresent madam had made that plain. Brad asked his visitor where he got his information.

Hara bowed slightly. "A friend in the composing room of the Mainichi. He thought I would be interested."

"Oh?" Eagerly, Brad leaned over the man. "Okay; I should care how. All I want to know is where she is."

"I'm sorry," Hara said, his English precise and stilted. "I do not know the whereabouts of Miss Kamiya. But I should like to offer my services. You will need an interpreter, a man who knows the city well."

Leave it to the Nippers, Brad thought. Let them smell a dollar, and they'll come running. Still, Hara was right; Brad would need help to sort the truth from rumors, the con men from people who actually knew something. This little guy looked and talked like a college professor down on his luck.

"For how much?" he asked.

Hara named a ridiculously low figure.

"You're hired," Brad said, and reached for the envelope with the return address. "Know where this is?"

Hara peered at the faded Oriental characters through his glasses. "We will find it."

With the help of a voluble cabbie, they did. The house was small, crowded by others, set far back on

18

an unpaved street. Brad stood at the gate while Hara rang the bell, and thought that this might be the place Sueko had played as a kid, the place she grew up. Before she had to go to work. And who the hell was he to censure her for turning prostitute? How else could a girl in Japan take care of a family then?

Brad tensed himself as the gate swung back. But a man stood in it, a man standing twisted because of a withered right leg, with bitter lines etched around his mouth and at the corners of his obsidian eyes. He flicked a glance at Brad, spat rapid Japanese at Mr. Hara. Hara answered politely, softly, while Brad shifted from one foot to the other. Dammit, did Sueko live here, or didn't she?

The man was staring fixedly at Brad now, thin lips curled, hating. What the hell, Brad wondered. He'd never seen the guy before; why all the dirty looks? Mr. Hara touched his arm.

"This is Kamiya Saburo, and this is his house."

"Kamiya?" Brad stuttered. "That's Sueko's last name. Who—her brother, maybe? Where is she? Where's Sueko?"

The man looked down at his withered leg, back up at Brad. In English, he said: "I don't know."

Brad stepped close. "Hell—you *must* know. Look, I'll pay you—plenty of money. Just tell me where she is. Isn't Sueko your sister? Look—I'll pay anything within reason. Just tell me—"

Saburo's face was flinty. "You Americans already paid me," he said savagely, and touched his crippled leg. "With this. Keep your dirty money. I tell you nothing."

Involuntarily, Brad's hands lifted to shake the information out of the sullen man. He stopped himself. Mr. Hara said something rapidly in Japanese; thin-voiced, Saburo answered him, hurling angry words. Then he hobbled back a few steps and slammed the gate. Brad heard a bolt slip into place on the other side. His legs tightened beneath him; his big

19

shoulders lowered, readying him to smash through the wood, to pound the answers out of the sneering man.

"Please," Hara said. "He will tell us nothing. A bitter man; a vengeful one."

"Why, dammit? What the hell did I ever do to him? I don't even know the guy; never saw him before. And is he related to Sueko?"

Hara nodded, led the way back to the waiting taxi. "Her brother, as you guessed. Why does he hate you? His leg—an American bombing raid. He was fourteen, and the planes also killed his father."

Brad slammed into the back seat of the cab. "That's *my* fault? Hell, you know better than that."

Small, composed, the little Japanese settled back, told the driver where to go. "Yes, Mr. Saxon—I know. Perhaps I know better than most. But to such a man, you are a symbol, something to blame, someone to hate. He would tell me nothing, because I was with you."

"Sueko's brother," Brad said. "She said something about him, and mentioned a sister, too."

But nothing about blaming every GI for her father's death, Brad remembered; nothing about how tough it was to live with everything gone. Uncomplaining, gentle, Sueko might have been a carefree schoolgirl. Except schoolgirls didn't work in the New Opal Hotel. Unless they had to.

"What now?" Brad asked. For some reason, he found himself liking Hara. The guy looked like a prototype of all Japanese, but there was something sturdy about him, something deep and sincere.

"The Namura," Hara said, "unless you wish to do something else?"

Brad clutched the back of the seat as the cab skidded dizzily around a corner. He told Hara about the New Opal, his hunch that a girl there knew something and was afraid to tell. It was only a hunch, he said, but possibly worth following up. Would Mr.

20

Hara take a room at the Namura, so he'd be handy? Brad would pay for it, of course. Mr. Hara would, happily.

Brad made arrangements for the room next to his, and they ate together in the hotel dining room. The food was excellent and well served. So were the pre-dinner martinis and the coffee-and-brandies, based, Brad knew, upon black market stock peddled by GIs and officers who got it dirt cheap.

All in the game, he thought, and eyed the crowded room, the string combo playing softly in one corner. Everybody sells, everybody busy. The Forty-Niners had bought his beef and muscle. He had bought a girl for the night, in the New Opal.

Almost like the one seated alone at the table over there. Smaller, though—a tiny Venus of jeweled parts; softer-looking than the girl at the table, too. Sueko had no lines around her mouth, no cynicism stamped upon her delicate face. A porcelain doll, shined and polished and put out for hire.

She'd been ashamed of being a virgin. Could you imagine that? *Ashamed,* dammit, because she didn't have the proper experience. She'd begged him not to tell the madam. A hell of a thing. And a stupid kid who didn't realize what he had. Kamiya Sueko. The names worked out as "The Last Flower in the Garden of the Gods," he found out later. And for a few lousy Yen, Brad Saxon had accomplished the deflowering.

Trembling and afraid, she'd been, and he thought it was an act, some phony setup she used to fool corny GIs. Until she was spread bare and face-hidden for him on the bed; until he ran his hands over the utter loveliness of her tiny, perfect body and came to her like some savage bull of a lonely field. Then he knew it was no act.

Later that night, he'd been gentle. In the dawn, they curled together like kittens in soft contentment, the young, hell-bent sergeant and the younger, just-

21

professional prostitute. She was so damned beautiful, so damned sweet—

"Mr. Saxon," Hara said. "The waiter wishes to know if you care for more brandy?"

Brad blinked, rubbed his face. "Yeah. Only not here. I want a couple of bottles set up. Hennessy: the good stuff."

Hara nodded. "I understand. The waiting is bad. Perhaps tomorrow—" remember?

"Perhaps tonight," Brad said, and took the check. "The New Opal, remember? Maybe you can talk the old lady there into saying something. Or the girl. But right now, I just want to crawl into a bottle and pull the cork after me."

At the exit, a youngster stepped in front of Brad. He was in civilian clothes, but the short hair and GI shoes marked him as Army. "Excuse me," he said, "I may be wrong but—aren't you Brad Saxon? From the Forty-Niners, I mean?"

Even here, Brad thought; but in a couple of years, nobody would remember. "Yes," he answered. "You from the Coast?"

"From the City," the boy said, as all San Franciscans call their town. "Man—I remember that game against the Rams where you—"

"Me, too. I've got the lumps to prove it."

There was more, with Mr. Hara standing patiently by, smiling to himself. Brad finally managed to break away from the fan, saying no, he was through playing ball, and sure, he was glad to meet somebody from home. But all he wanted was eight or nine big drinks, so he could stop remembering how it had been, with Sueko.

"An athlete," Mr. Hara said in the elevator. "I thought so."

"Sure," Brad said. "Look at the footprints on me. Look—I'll call you tonight; the New Opal is shut up until then. If we don't find anything there, we'll just have to wait until the ad stirs something up."

22

"Yes," Mr. Hara agreed, and went into his room.

Brad keyed his own door and went in, too. The girl was waiting for him inside, looking as if she belonged on his bed. All she wore was a thin kimono—open down the middle.

CHAPTER III

"*Kum-ba-wa,*" she said, which was, Brad figured, as good a way as any to greet a strange man from his own bed.

"Good evening," he answered politely. What the hell else did a guy say to that much exposed rose-and-ivory skin?

The woman stretched, arching fine breasts and sliding one tapered leg in his direction. Her hair puddled the white pillow like liquid ebony. The translucent kimono didn't cover much, but it evidently wasn't intended to.

Guiltily, Brad flinched at the sharp rapping on the door behind him.

"Your brandy, sir," the voice said.

Brad fumbled for the knob, blocked the door crack with his bulk as he fed the bellhop wadded Yen notes and snatched the whisky. When he turned back to the room, the woman had pulled herself together, drawn the loose robe about her. It was a damned shame.

He carried the tray to a table—brandy, ice, mixer, wondering if every available Japanese woman he saw was going to do this to him, send the blood racing through his body, urge him with the silken texture of her flesh. If so, he was in for a hell of a time. Ninety percent of the women here were available.

"I am Katsue," the woman said, moving from the bed in a fluid, entrancing motion, and coming to stand close to him. She took the brandy bottle from him, broke the seal expertly and poured two over the rocks.

"What is this?" Brad asked. "A service of the hotel?"

"*Nan-deska?*" she said, frowning. "No understand. I come to see you."

Damn, he thought. This Sueko thing must be pushing him harder than he knew. The woman here, this Katsue, seemed even more like his Sueko than any of the others. Something about the shape of the face, the tone of voice, the richness of her midnight hair and the innate grace with which she walked—

But it couldn't be. He was seeing Sueko in all women, overlapping her image upon the features of all women. Brad drained his glass. Katsue refilled it with the quick anticipation of the trained *Geisha*.

Brad moved away from her nearness, sat in the overstuffed chair, his weight making it creak. "All right," he said, "you wanted to see me. Take it from there."

Her face was flushed, and he remembered that Oriental women couldn't really drink; powerful American whisky jolted them in a hurry. Katsue flicked a pink tongue over ripe lips.

"The *shinbun*," she said, "the newspaper."

Brad choked on his drink. "What the hell? Does everybody in Tokyo have a friend on the Mainichi? That ad won't be out until tomorrow."

"I hear," Katsue said imperturbably. "Hundred dollars, okay?"

Brad emptied his glass, settled back in the chair. The girl had an angle, he supposed. Get in here with some hint that she knew things, that she could lead him straight to the woman he sought, and meanwhile peddle her very attractive wares.

"I'll pay a hundred dollar reward," he said, "or more. *If* you can prove your information is okay. What do you know about Kamiya Sueko?"

Katsue put down her glass, swayed a bit. "I know, okay. Damn right I know. You think I'm crook, *ne?*

I tell you about Sueko, okay. She's—twenty-seven; more small than me, *sukoshi* girl."

Right, Brad thought, with rising excitement. Sueko would be twenty-seven now. It was strange how he kept remembering her as eighteen.

"And?" Brad said eagerly. "And?"

Katsue fumbled with the kimono sash, whipped it back and away. One manicured fingernail pointed to a spot just below her right hipbone, made a tiny circle upon the bare golden flesh. "Mark here, *ne*? Funny mark."

Brad swallowed hard. Sure, Sueko had a birthmark there—a cute, mothlike outline. They had joked about it, laughed over it in those sweetward hours coiled spent and drained upon the soft *futon*, feeling the tingly silk of the bedding upon their nude bodies, feeling the greater tingle of delightfully familiar flesh touching hip to thigh, knee to knee.

"Where is she?" Brad asked. "Quick, damn you—where is she?"

Katsue giggled, splashed more brandy into her glass. She didn't bother to close the kimono; light glinted from her rounded thigh, from the swell of her calf. Brad came catlike to his feet, reached her in two swift steps, caught at her shoulders. Her flesh was warm under his palms.

"No hurry," Katsue said. "Nine years, *ne*? You wait more *sukoshi*—little bit more."

The girl tilted her glass, spilled amber drops across her chin. One trickled down her throat, came to rest diamonding the dusky valley between her erect breasts. Brad wanted to shake her, to squeeze her until the information he needed squirted from her like seeds from an orange. But she might lie. She had reasons for coming here as she had—reasons a Caucasian might not understand, but which probably made very good sense to her. Brad had learned that much about the Orient.

She twisted under his hands to place the glass on

the table, twisted back to flatten her writhing body tightly to him, wet mouth lifted, eyes slumberous. He kissed her, hard and long and searching.

Katsue lifted herself, struggled to crawl through his clothing and into his pores, to blend and mix her straining flesh with his own. Head spinning, Brad carried her toward the bed.

Her hands were frantic at his clothes, the soles of her feet gripping his calves like eager hands. The woman was a seething cauldron, driving, sinuous, an uncontrolled passion that sought as much to destroy as to soothe. They locked together in a battle, thoughtless, senseless. It raged through and around them. Neither of them won.

Angry at himself, Brad pulled away from the girl, thrust his blocky, powerful legs into his pants. The old wound behind his knee twinged. He stalked bare-chested to the brandy and helped himself. He didn't turn when he heard the swift patter of feet heading for the bath, eyed his glass moodily as the water purled behind a closed door. So the girl had gotten what she wanted, earned whatever bonus she thought it was worth. When she came out of the shower, she was going to tell him about Sueko—or wish she had.

Katsue was glowing, freshened; cold water had cleared her eyes. It hadn't done anything to the de-termined set of her mouth. "Hundred dollars?" she reminded him, and added: "Five dollars more."

Brad snorted, pawed at his hip and brought out his wallet. Her eyes followed it greedily. "Have green money?" she asked.

"No," he said.

No "green money," for this girl, or anyone else in Japan. Sure, it brought double its face value. But it also slipped from hand to hand, traveled far and fast, until it came to rest beyond the Yalu River in Red China—or went even farther, to Russia. From there, payments went out for vital war materials, to make paychecks for spies and fellow travelers, to grease hands at borders where American dollars were always good.

"No green money," he repeated, and brought out thousand-Yen notes. Katsue watched, shrugged and put out a hand. Brad drew the money to him. "Where's Sueko?"

Her dark eyes fastened to his. "You speak hundred dollars. You pay—even if no can find Sueko?"

"The ad reads: 'for information leading to her,'" Brad said. "You'll earn the money, if you can tell me anything important. You've proven you know her. Now, dammit—tell me!"

A faintly elusive smile played over Katsue's mouth, not reaching the fixedness of her eyes. "Dead," she said, as if she enjoyed the taste of the word.

Brad felt the blood drain from his face, felt a cold, hard knot twist itself deep in his belly. "You're lying!"

She had to be lying. Sueko dead? It couldn't be—not that dainty, magnificent body; not that flower petal face; not the love and scent and feel of her. No.

Of its own volition, a big hand flashed out, crunched its fingers into Katsue's upper arm. The girl's mouth snapped open in terror mixed with an underlying hate. She spat the words at him: "Sueko dead—damn you! I tell you she's dead. I know!"

Convulsively, Brad flung her from him. Katsue tried to catch her balance, fell sprawling across the bed with her naked legs flailing. Rolling over, she glared up at the huge man towering white-faced over her.

"You know," Brad mumbled through numb lips. "You know. *How* do you know?"

She inched across the bed, scuttling slowly back from the wild hurt in his face, from the hint of a great rage threatening to explode in blind destruction, from this coiling man who was about to rip and tear and

28

hammer because a precious thing had been taken from him.

"I know," she mumbled, "because I am Kamiya Katsue—her sister."

CHAPTER IV

He was into the second bottle of Hennessy, and it wasn't doing a hell of a lot of good. It kept him from kicking holes in the walls. Its narcotic effect stopped him from ripping apart the furniture. But that was all. No welcome blackout, where he couldn't think and feel.

Brad had seen the identity card all prostitutes in Japan are forced to carry. The name on it was Kamiya Katsue; the address the same one he had visited earlier in the day. First the embittered brother, crippled and sullen; then Katsue, whose greed came before anything else. Well, she'd earned her damned blood money.

Another long drink slid down Brad's throat. Hell—he couldn't even put flowers on Sueko's grave. Cremated, Katsue said. The ashes scattered into Tokyo Bay. Hell. He drank again. And again, until the dark curtain closed down around him.

Mr. Hara had rapped several times upon the door, listening between knocks. Finally, he glanced quickly up and down the hallway, and brought out a flat key. He worked it into the lock and slid deftly inside Brad's room. He nodded at the sight of the big man stretched limp and sweating upon the bed, and eased to his wallet.

The little Japanese thumbed through the billfold, pausing at cards, pursing his lips at the passport. Carefully, he replaced the wallet on its former spot on the table. He didn't take any money. He went through pockets of the suits hanging in the closet, searched between shirts and underwear in the dresser drawers. Then he went out as softly as he had come, closing and locking the door behind him. Mr. Hara didn't turn into his own room, but instead moved down the stairs and out into the street. A dark, plain car pulled up at the curb and he ducked into it to be whisked away.

It must have been midnight when the burly man in uniform thumped Brad's door. Brad stirred, muttered, and flung out one arm. The hammering continued, officious, demanding. Brad forced his eyes open and cursed.

The voice was American, rough and husky, used to command. "Saxon? I know you're in there. Open up!"

Brad sat up, rubbed bleary eyes, tasted green fuzz inside his mouth. He washed away the taste with a mixture of melted ice and brandy. The pounding continued. Brad didn't like it.

"Get the hell away from that door," he said.

"Open up. This is Captain Getty—Military Police!"

Reflex action lifted Brad to his feet and across the room, where he turned the knob before he remembered he was a civilian, that the MPs didn't have a damned thing to do with him, one way or another.

"So?" he said into the beefy red face.

The man was big—almost as large as Brad himself, but he'd gone to seed. A double roll of flesh bulged beneath his craggy chin; dark pouches sagged his eyes, and a swollen belly pushed at a too-small belt. The uniform was neat, the crossed pistols on its collar brightly polished. Houseboys, Brad thought, were handy to have around.

"May I come in?" Getty asked.

"I thought you'd never ask," Brad said, and turned away. Getty followed him into the room, ID folder open in one sweaty hand. Brad glanced at it and

31

looked back to the bottle. He'd have to wake up room service and order another, he decided.

"We understand you're in Tokyo looking for a certain girl," the captain said.

Brad didn't offer him a drink. "You a stockholder on the newspaper? You might as well join the party. So what about it?"

Getty brought out a cigar, thumbed its cellophane away and stuck it between square teeth. He didn't light it. "As an ex-soldier, you should know we have ways of obtaining information. It doesn't matter how we know."

Brad decided abruptly that he wanted no part of this fat slob, brass pistols and all. He said it slowly: "I thought that 'we' routine went out when the Great White Father got shanghaied from over here. You a leftover from his cabinet?"

Getty reddened, eyes bulging. "No need to take that attitude, Saxon. We—I—realize you're a civilian, now."

Jaw muscles tightening, Brad stared at the captain. "Make sure you do, buster. And the name is *Mister* Saxon, get it? Now say whatever the hell you came busting into my room to say, then haul it out of here and go shake down some business girl."

The MP sputtered; veins stood out in his swollen throat. "Look here—"

One outthrust finger trip-hammered into Getty's chest, banged hard and repeatedly against his collarbone. "*You* look," Brad said, pushing, hoping the man would push back. "This is my room; Japan is a friendly country now; you and the MPs can go blow your tin whistles. You going to deliver your message before I throw you down the stairs?"

Paling, Getty moved back a step, and then another. "I—I came to—help you, dammit. The girl you're looking for is dead. She died two years ago, according to our files."

32

Brad set himself. "And what was her name doing in MP files?"

The captain blinked rapidly, tried to recover his dignity, his tone of command. "Surely you know what she was. All prostitutes are registered. And—there were other things."

"What other things?"

Getty was sweating. "Black market; suspicion of thefts; consorting with known communists. She had quite a dossier."

"You're a damned liar. Sueko wouldn't steal a dime. And she hated the Reds just as I did."

"We—I—don't want to break security, but she was all I said. A trouble-maker, a headache to the Japanese police as well."

Brad frowned, moved closer. "And you came here in the middle of the night, just to tell me all this? You came here out of the goodness of your heart, because you wanted to help an ex-GI far from home? The hell you did, captain. Now spit out the rest of it before I run up one side of you and down the other."

Getty's small, pouched eyes turned mean. "Go ahead; I'd like to get you slammed into a Jap jail where friends of mine can get at you. I know your type, Saxon—a big shot football player, big wheel on the sports pages. You were nothing but a lousy sergeant in the Army. Go ahead—try roughing me up and see what happens."

Softly, dangerously, Brad hissed the words: "Sure, you've got connections. A slob like you exists on connections. I'll bet you even know somebody in the ambassador's office, don't you? Some cheap clerk who could get my visa yanked. I don't doubt that—captain. I'm not even interested. But I *am* interested in you. I want to find out how many times you'll bounce."

Getty back-pedaled, squeaking. Low and sudden, Brad's blocking shoulder thudded into the soft belly, hurled the gasping captain into the wall. Brad dug

33

his feet into the floor, kept the man pinned there for a long moment. Then he slipped aside and allowed the breathless Getty to slide to the carpet where he held his stomach and sucked for air.

"You don't bounce so well," Brad said.

"D-damn you—"

"I'll wait right here," Brad said, "while you go tell your friends to make me *persona non grata* in this country. But you'd better have the CIC do a little more checking up. Tell them to nose around the State Department."

He'd said the magic words. A flicker of fear crossed Getty's face. He could almost see the man's mind working furiously, going over any information he had on Brad Saxon, not finding anything concerning the State Department, but afraid to make a mistake that could cost him his bars.

Brad hooked a hand into Getty's shirtfront, effortlessly jerked the captain to his feet. "I don't know why you came here," he said, "and I don't give a damn if your connections reach all the way into the Imperial Palace. I do know you lied about Sueko, and that you're damned anxious to get me out of Tokyo. Now hear me well, fat boy—I'm going to find out things. And if you get in my way, officially or unofficially, I'm going to bust you right in half."

He flung the captain toward the door. Getty pawed at the knob, struggled for a shred of composure. He started to say something, but thought better of it when Brad lifted both hands eagerly. Getty snatched the door wide and plunged through it into the hall. He almost ran over the little Japanese standing there.

"Get the hell outa' my way," Getty snarled, and shoved the small man roughly aside. Brad heard his boots thumping hard against the carpeted stairs, and thought the MP enlisted men would catch hell tonight.

"Please?" Mr. Hara said. "I heard shouting. May I be of help?"

34

"Come on in," Brad said. "I was just about to send down for another jug. You can help me with it."

Hara drifted in, closed the door softly. "American liquor is too strong for me."

"Tonight it's like water," Brad said, and proved it by downing a glassful. "I didn't have time to introduce you to the MP captain—but then, he's not a guy you'd like to know, anyway."

Mr. Hara sat gingerly upon a chair, hands folded. "*Ah-so?* Perhaps he had information?"

Brad shook his head. "He told me the same thing the girl did—that Sueko is—dead." The word was difficult to say. Brad went on. "He also hinted strongly that he'd have me worked over if I didn't take my big nose out of Japan. Now what the hell do you suppose all that was about?"

"I have heard of this captain," Hara said. "A dangerous enemy."

"A jerk," Brad corrected. "I'm not worried about him. His boys didn't dig deep enough into my background. I have a friend or two, myself. My father is —well, pretty high up in the State Department. He wouldn't like it if I got myself into a jam over here, but he'd pull me out. But I'd just like to know why a jerk like Getty is involved in this. And why. Why did he bother to come here to tell me Sueko is dead? And why all the lies about her?"

If they *were* lies. Brad thought. Nine years could bring a lot of changes in a girl who had to scrape for a living. Especially one who had been deserted by the man she thought loved her; her first man. Who the hell could blame Sueko for doing anything—pushing heroin, trading on the black market, even for peddling bits of information gleaned from big-mouthed GIs to local communist bosses?

But if she was dead, as two people said—why the interest in her? Katsue, Brad could understand. The girl would sell what was left of her soul for a few bucks. Probably Captain Getty would, too. Yet the fat MP officer hadn't even mentioned money. Therefore, it figured that he was being paid from some other source. Who? and again—why?

Brad gulped more brandy and turned to ask Mr. Hara these questions. The little man beat him to the punch. "Mr. Saxon—I think that Kamiya Sueko is not dead. I think she is very much alive."

CHAPTER V

After the first few attempts at sorting reports from the crowd of applicants who'd answered his ad, Brad gave up and turned the problem over to Mr. Hara. From across the room, he watched the efficient little interpreter listen, take notes, and dismiss a long line of people who claimed to know Sueko.

And several Sueko Kamiyas themselves showed up. The name wasn't rare, and neither were the girls who wore it into Brad's suite. They were alike in cheap skirts and cheaper sweaters, imitation bobbysoxers who would have looked far better in their native kimonos. But they were nothing like the real Sueko.

Or were they, Brad wondered. Time and trouble might have made many changes in the girl he'd known, turned her into a sleazy carbon copy of girls in a thousand ports—hard and brittle women who'd forgotten the meaning of love, if they'd ever known it.

He also thought about Hara's hunch that Sueko wasn't dead. A hunch was all the idea could be, but it had sounded far stronger than that, as if the man was somehow certain. Of course, the little guy might just be stretching out his job, making it last. Brad frowned out of the window; no—Hara wasn't a con artist. If he was, he was so good that he was wasting his time on a small operation.

Brad stared out over a section of the city—the largest in the world, more crowded, more desperate. Somewhere among that jumble of modern buildings and pagoda roofs, there was the girl he'd come to find.

Or if not here, in some other town—Yokohoma, Kobe, Sasebo, Fukuoaka. Wherever Sueko was, he'd find her. He'd only started; there were TV stations, radios —other newspapers both in English and Japanese. There were detectives here, too. Brad would find her —or what was left of her. He wouldn't stop until he did.

The back of his left knee ached momentarily, and Brad stooped to knead it. He'd cursed that knee at first—the bullet that started its trickiness, then the twisting and banging it got on the field.

It had slowed him a little, as the years passed. Not enough to make him a cripple, but enough to make him a split-second late on plays, to throw him a half-step behind the line action, weakening at the damndest times.

And it had finally made him quit football. Oh, he could have put up with it for a few more years, using his stubborn power to make up for lack of mobility, warming the bench a lot, maybe eventually drifting into a line coach's slot. But Brad figured it was time to bow out while he was still remembered as a pretty good tackle. And the investments had made him independent.

So now he felt a sort of blessed attachment to the trick knee. Without it, he might have gone on battering skulls with opposing linemen for a long time. Without it, he might not have had time to think about going back to Japan, nor gotten up the nerve.

Brad flexed his leg, gave the bum knee an affectionate pat, and glanced at his watch. "Hara?"

The little man turned from a table, wearily motioning away the latest reward claimant. "Yes?"

"We had a long night. Let's eat and sleep awhile. Then we'll go check out the New Opal. I'll hire another room off the lobby, pay some clerk to interview the rest of those people."

Hara sighed. "If you wish. Shall I see to the arrangements?"

"Please. You'll be ready to go, tonight?"

Hara bowed. "I am always ready."

Brad frowned after the man as he went out. Schoolteacher? Small businessman in tough times? More likely a former high-ranking officer of the Imperial forces. There was something about him—

It was a bit early when they stood before the New Opal, but not early enough for the place to be tightly closed. Brad pounded on the door again. No answer, although he heard someone stirring inside. He looked at Mr. Hara; the Japanese shrugged, lifted both palms helplessly.

"Oh no," Brad muttered. He was more than a little tired of getting the Oriental run-around. He wanted to talk to the girl behind those doors, wanted to find out what made Machiko's eyes flicker in fear when he mentioned Sueko's name.

And he was going to.

Brad moved back to the curb, crossed his arms in front of his face, and hurled his two hundred and thirty pounds savagely forward. He went through the thin wood and glass with a roar of exploding panels and shattering panes, scattered two small tables and several chairs, and ended against the bar with a slam that shook bottles off the shelves behind it.

There was a faint smile on Mr. Hara's mouth as he picked his way gingerly through the debris and followed the big man across the courtyard. Another locked door. Brad fisted a hole through this one so he could get a grip on its frame. Then he tore it off its sliding racks and flung it into the fence. A girl yipped, far back in the house.

"Machiko!" Brad yelled. "Machiko!"

He strode down the hallway, jerking doors wide and peering into rooms. "Machiko!"

Brad found her in the familiar room, the one they'd shared together, the never-forgotten room that had once been lighted by the aura of Sueko. He found Machiko there, and wished he hadn't.

39

Mr. Hara pattered up to Brad's elbow, and sucked in his breath with a hiss. Slowly, Brad moved into the room, kneeled beside the stained bed. "Machiko—can you hear me?"

Tiny, whimpering sounds worked their way past swollen, bleeding lips. The girl moaned, tried to lift her head from the pillow. One eye was split and closed; a brutal fist had glanced off the cheekbone below the other, flattening the bone but missing the eye. Machiko had been mauled, terribly and methodically. Her open eye was glazed with agony and horror; a tear trembled on its lower lash.

"Machiko," Brad said, "did they do this to you because of me? The questions I asked?"

The tear slid onto her distorted cheekbone and dissolved. Painfully, the girl's head moved from side to side. Through clenched teeth, Brad cursed, whispery and outraged. A soft and gentle girl like this—

Suddenly Hara was beside her, speaking swiftly in their own language, a folded letter in one hand. Brad saw Machiko's good eye move to it, saw her nod and try to sob. He grabbed Hara's shoulder.

"What's that?"

Hara's face was drawn, sick. "A letter that came while you slept. From her. She wanted to tell you something."

"And somebody found out," Brad said. "I'll tear this damned place down around their ears—"

"The girl is badly beaten," Hara said. "We must get her to a hospital. Then I will help you tear down this place."

"Call a hospital," Brad said. "I'll stay with her until—"

The madam screamed from the hall—harsh-voiced, accusing. Her hand pointed at Brad and the girl. Feet pattered, another girl screamed. Hara tried to shout over the madam's banshee keening, to explain. A man shouted from the courtyard. Faces appeared behind the madam—men's faces, set and angry. Brad

40

flicked a glance at Machiko and moved out to meet them, moved to keep them in the hall and courtyard and away from the girl.

Squawking, the madam fled. As Brad's great shoulders filled the hall, the two men drifted back for the courtyard. He stalked them, big hands stretched, head pulled in and low, eyes timing their movements from beneath shaggy, scarred brows. They backed from the ripped-away door and into the open. Brad followed them, marking the way they spread apart to come at him from two sides. Watching them, he didn't see the one waiting beside the door.

The club caught him across the top of his head. Its broken end bounced off the flagstones. Brad shook the blur from his eyes and lunged to his left, spinning in time to catch the shortened club as it slammed down for another blow. He caught the man's wrist and snatched it across his body. Running tiptoe and startled, the man was jerked forward to meet the stunning smash of a driving kneecap. His yelp was drowned by a spray of blood and broken teeth. Brad chopped him across the back of the neck as he fell.

A man hit him over the eye, in the mouth, with swift, cutting punches. Brad turned, lowered his head and drove forward, with arms spread wide. The top of his head found a target—soft flesh, the arch of ribs. The man fell away, bounced the head back into the fence, hooked it again, and as the pale face tried to fall, pivoted to bring his elbow into it with the full force of his weight. Things crunched and broke.

Lips peeled back in savage joy, Brad whirled to find the third man. He was down already, with Mr. Hara's childlike foot across his neck. Brad straightened up, sucked great gulps of air into his heaving chest. Another surprise from the ubiquitous Mr. Hara. The little guy didn't look as if he could break out of a cigaret pack.

"Your boy looks in better shape," Brad grunted. "Let's see if he can answer some questions."

41

Hara brushed his parchment hands together. "A pleasure."

But there wasn't time. A siren whined to a stop outside the New Opal; whistles shrilled. Blood pumping, eager to do battle, Brad braced himself to meet the police. Mr. Hara tugged at his sleeve, said things about a jail being no place to find Sueko, and Brad subsided.

Captain Getty was the fifth man into the courtyard. Two MPs and a pair of Japanese police had run interference for him. The policemen had guns in their hands; the MPs balanced wary clubs. Getty glanced around, grinning.

"Couldn't take a little advice, eh, Saxon?"

The madam screeched out of the house, spitting and snarling, her painted face a mask of rage. Hara stared at her, eyes alert behind his rimless glasses. The police listened; one took notes while the other interpreted for the waiting MP captain.

Getty's wet smile widened. "So you beat hell out of a girl, too? You won't like the jail, Saxon. Remember what I told you about my friends there?"

Brad took a step forward. "*Mister* Saxon, I told you, slob. And I figure the only friends you've got live in pigpens."

One of the MPs turned aside, his shoulders quivering. The other one was young and a little frightened. Getty chopped the air with a beefy hand. "Bring them in. We'll see how wise they are in the station."

Brad touched Mr. Hara. "Tell the old bat I'll be back; and ask your cops to get an ambulance for Machiko."

Rapidly, Hara said it before the police escorted them both to cars at the curb. They had to push through a curious, scowling crowd. Brad settled back on the seat. Mr. Hara didn't seem a damned bit worried, as most Japanese would be in the hands of the police. Okay then, neither was Brad Saxon.

Getty couldn't do a damned thing, no matter how

much the fat boy bragged and blustered. The military didn't have a finger in this. Sure, Getty could drop a word here and there, maybe get Brad worked over in a remote station house. But Brad thought money would speak a lot louder than any words from Captain Getty. He'd buy his way out of trouble, because money talked anywhere in the world. Only here in the Orient, it shouted.

Had they reached another dead end? Brad didn't think so. He and Hara had just run into some more interesting people—men and women who tried to keep him from learning anything about Sueko. The madam and her bouncers had put some effort into it. Brad grinned. The old witch would have to hire some new boys; the old ones wouldn't be much good for some time to come.

The woman had been desperate enough to sick the cops on him with her lies about Brad beating Machiko. Her toughs had attempted to put him away. Brad felt the knot on his head. The guy with the club hadn't been kidding. But hell—what kind of tackle couldn't take a pop on the skull? Even the water-boy for the Forty-Niners could shake that off.

Brad looked over at the imperturbable Mr. Hara. The little guy handled himself okay; probably a black-belt Judo fanatic. Brad wondered how that would work if the going got tougher. It probably would, next time. Somebody was anxious as all hell to keep Brad away from Sueko Kamiya.

Cautiously, the Japanese police stood aside and motioned Brad and Hara into the station. Getty's MP jeep was just pulling up. Brad touched his inside pocket, found the wallet there and walked up the grimy stone steps into district police headquarters.

Mr. Hara had a wallet, too, and brought it out swiftly, his back cutting off Brad's view as the little man spoke rapidly in Japanese. A lieutenant answered—deferentially, Brad thought in surprise. More

43

hurried dialog, and Captain Getty waddled into the station.

"Hey, Keijo," Getty said, and the police lieutenant bit his lips and looked up.

"Take care of this pair," Getty continued. "The Army's not interested in 'em—know what I mean? Wouldn't surprise me if you could lose 'em for a couple of weeks, and they wouldn't be missed any. The big one damned near killed a little Japanese girl; your boys ought to teach him a lesson, eh?"

Malevolently, Getty sneered at Brad. "These guys don't read much about big-wheel football players, Saxon. Now if you were a Yankee shortstop—"

Tensely, the police lieutenant said: "Captain—we will investigate."

Getty blinked. "Huh? Listen, Keijo—"

"Yamata," the man corrected. "Lieutenant Yamata, captain. I will take charge of the prisoners now."

"Hey," Getty blustered. "Listen here—this is your old buddy talkin'. You forgettin' about the times we —"

Yamata got up from the desk and turned his back on Getty. The MP captain's fleshy jaw sagged. "Okay," he said. "Okay—I'll remember this. You can bet I'll damned well remember this."

Brad wasn't certain what was going on, but he couldn't resist throwing the hooks into Getty as the redfaced man stamped past him for the door. "Friend of yours, captain?"

Getty snarled. "I'm not through with you, Saxon. I'll see you run out of Japan yet."

"I'm not through with you, either," Brad said softly. "I promised I'd break you into little pieces if you got in my way again. I intend to keep that promise, fat boy."

Mr. Hara slid deftly between them, blinking through his glasses. "All a mistake, Mr. Saxon. The police ask you accept their apologies."

Getty plunged out of the station, snorting. Brad

44

lifted an eyebrow at Hara. "You'll have to explain this to me. I've been around Japan long enough and often enough to know that nobody—I repeat—*nobody*, gets released this quickly, without even an investigation."

Hara inclined his head. "I will explain, but outside please; in the taxi that will take us to the hospital."

"To see Machiko?"

"Of course. And for the sake of the captain's 'old buddy'—she had better be there by now."

Brad massaged the bump atop his head and followed Hara out. There was a hell of a lot more to this little guy than met the eye. Another stumbling block being thrown in Brad's way? More trickery to keep him from finding Sueko?

In the cab, Brad decided against the ideas. Hara had been too helpful; he was on Brad's side, and Brad was glad he was. Anybody who could snap a police lieutenant to attention like a rubber band was a good ally. But why was Hara helping?

He asked the man.

"Mr. Saxon," Hara said, "You will forgive me for not explaining before this, but I had to be certain you were what you seemed. Japan is an uneasy country these days, no matter how it seems on the surface. There are problems, you understand—"

"No, dammit," Brad said. "I *don't* understand, and I'm not too interested in Japan's problems, either. I came here to find a girl—for personal reasons. Personal reasons, hell! Because I love her, and I'm going to marry her and take her back with me if I have to whip the entire island of Honshu—with the American Army thrown in!"

It was the first time he'd heard Mr. Hara laugh aloud. "And I believe you would, Mr. Saxon," the Japanese chuckled, then turning serious, he added: "But we are as anxious to have you reach your love as you are. Only it must be on our terms."

Mr. Hara nodded. "*We*—the secret police."

45

CHAPTER VI

In a daze, Brad wandered across the Nomura's lobby. Everybody was getting into the act—MPs, thugs, madams, and now the Japanese Secret Police. Mr. Hara had been explicit about that. He'd been definite at the police station, too, getting them sprung in a hurry. No wonder the cops had jumped. Hara's job was comparable to a like position in the US Security Agency—big time, big boys who played for keeps.

Brad ignored the waiting elevator and climbed the stairs, thinking. At the hospital, Machiko had been close to coma, and couldn't tell them much. She'd managed to repeat a couple of names—names they already knew: Saburo and Katsue Kamiya. Maybe she had more information, but they'd have to wait for it. She was a sick girl.

Every time Brad thought of the beating she'd taken, his stomach muscles tightened, and there was a bitter taste in his mouth. He wished he'd killed the thugs who jumped him in the courtyard of the New Opal. But Hara was getting a rundown on them, and on the wily madam who hired them. His orders to Brad were simple: stay put until you hear from me.

Brad moved quietly down the hall to his room, reached for the key. His nerves were taut, and he was still jumpy, on edge. At the door, he paused, listening. And heard a faint rattling in the room beyond. Brad eased the key into the lock, turned it very slowly, carefully.

The man didn't know he was there until Brad shut

46

the door and leaned against it. The click spun him around, staring.

"If you don't know English, buster," Brad said, "you'd better learn it in a hurry."

The Oriental was tense, balanced ready to leap.

"I hope you do," Brad said.

The man relaxed, slowly spread empty hands. "No trouble."

"You already made it, buster. You bet I can't kick you out the window before you get a hand in that pocket?"

"Easy," the man said. "I've seen you in action before, Saxon. Play it cool and I'll talk it up."

Brad stared. "You're no Nipper."

"In a way—maybe three generations back. I'm Johnny Kojima—a Forty-Niner fan. Think they'll make it this year?"

Brad took a step forward. "You get a ticket to search my room?"

Kojima hesitated, then shook his head. "Maybe I better tag 'lieutenant' to my name. CIC."

"And what the hell has Counter Intelligence got to do with me?"

"Like you say, nothing with *you.*" Kojima's grin was catchy. He looked like the Nisei kids around the campuses of San Francisco College and San Jose State—bright and alert, but ready to clam up if they know a guy and accept him.

"So?"

"Orders, Saxon. Don't blame me. Seems a lot of people are nosy about your ex-girlfriend—Miss Kamiya."

"Including you."

"Orders, remember? You won't say anything about this? Headquarters might make me turn in my cloak and dagger for getting caught flat-footed."

Brad didn't move. "Reach just two fingers into your coat; pull out your ID—slow. Drop it on the table and back off."

Kojima grinned. "Like the book says."

The ID folder was in mid-air when Brad was on the man, amazingly fast for a man of his bulk. One hand spun Kojima around and held him motionless. The other darted into an inside coat pocket and snatched out a .38 with a two-inch barrel. Brad shoved the man onto the couch.

Then he scanned the ID folder and flipped it back. He held the gun. "Okay—so you're CIC. Getty send you up here?"

Kojima grimaced. "That clown? Can I have my pistol back? It's kind of embarrassing, you know."

Brad tossed it to him. Kojima slid it back into his coat. "Some day I'm going to start practicing my quick draw."

"Look," Brad said, crossing to the brandy bottle. "I'm getting up to here with mysterious guys stumbling around in my business. First Getty leans on me, then I get mouse-trapped by three Fu Manchu types, then the Secret Police—"

Kojima looked at the door, put a finger to his lips. "Easy. Mr. Hara might not like that to get around."

"You know about him?"

"We know."

"Then tell *me*," Brad said, irritated. "I'm the only guy running blind around here, and I'm liable to start running right over people."

The CIC agent shook his head as Brad offered brandy. "I can tell you that we're on your side—or more like right behind you. You're a civilian with a few strings to pull. You can go places we can't, bull-doze your way through slobs we have to step easy around. My outfit is just following along and sorting out the wreckage."

"And Hara?"

"A sharp fortune cookie; he's in this for reasons of his own."

Brad swallowed a drink. "One more thing, Johnny —a girl named Sueko."

48

Johnny Kojima rubbed his chin. "We don't know for sure, but you might be disappointed, Brad. You've been away a long time."

"Not that long," Brad said. "Not that damned long."

Kojima stood up. "Okay; let it stand at that. I hope you find her pretty quick, guy."

Brad frowned. "Don't you know where she is?"

"No. We're depending on you to find her."

"For you—or for me?"

Kojima turned at the door. "That depends on how deep she's mixed up in things."

"The hell it does," Brad said. "You told me, now I'm telling you and the CIC. Keep your hands off that girl until I've talked to her."

Kojima grinned again. "*Me*, yes. You better Hong-Kong believe it, as the sage said. You damned near broke my arm already. I left ⸬ card on the couch. You might want to get in touch."

He was gone, leaving Brad to stare at a blank door. A good kid, Brad thought, and a shrewd one, too. Kojima probably could have potted him with that .38 when he came into the room. No big, ugly tackle was fast enough to cross a room *that* quickly. He'd be a halfback, if he could.

Brad picked the card off the couch, and turned it over. On the back, pencilled very lightly, were four words: "Yokohama Sex Drug Store." Brad's eyebrows pulled down. Sex Drug Store? Something about that —he snapped his fingers, remembering. Yes—those wild ads in English-language newspapers like the Japan Times. How'd they go? "Biggest and best all-sex drug store in Japan . . . all desires, all problems . . ." Something like that. The GIs had gotten a hell of a belt out of the ads, used to mail them home as souvenirs.

He looked at the card again. Just a telephone number on the front; the drug store note on the reverse. What the hell? Johnny Kojima had said Brad could go places and bulldoze people the CIC couldn't

49

touch. A lead for Brad to follow? A hint of how to go about it?

Sure. Tossing off another quick brandy, Brad whipped into the shower. He changed into a light-weight suit and clean shirt, open at the throat. He was halfway to the door before he remembered. Mr. Hara said stay put until further notice. Brad hesitated.

Let Mr. Hara go pound *suki-yaki*, he decided. Yokohama wasn't far away, and maybe—maybe Sueko was there!

CHAPTER VII

Brad hung onto the back of the driver's seat, and occasionally closed his eyes tightly as the little taxi whizzed over the Tokyo-Yokohama highway, brushing carts and bicycles, and scattering unwary pedestrians.

On an open stretch, he sat back and forced himself to think of other things. Like Sueko, and the remembered taste and feel of her. Other patients at the hospital had kidded him about his every-night passes into town, about his obvious eagerness to leave for the weekend.

"Shackrat," they said, some enviously, some cynically, and asked how his shackmate was doing.

Had it been that—the half-sneering acceptance of a different moral code? Maybe it was the too-wise looks, the knowledge of cash-on-the-line love. Sure, the CIs said—you slept with them, because they were the best bed-partners anywhere. But you didn't marry them, by a damned sight.

All the while, blithely ignoring the fact that almost a hundred American soldiers each week were doing just that—marrying their shackmates, their "onlies," their prostitute girlfriends. Not Brad Saxon, of course. Not the guy raised on Knob Hill, with the omnipresent shadow of duty and international affairs ever looming over him.

No, not young, stiffnecked Brad Saxon. He was going to accept all she gave so freely—the velvet legs, the cushioning breasts, the enchanted depths and cur-

51

rents of Sueko. Then he was going to flip it off with a *sayonara,* kiss her goodbye without regrets, and hop aboard the big bird that would carry him back to the States—and the kind of life a Japanese girl just wouldn't fit into.

Only he lost his nerve, when the time came. He didn't tell her goodbye. He let her think he'd be back as usual, that nothing had changed for them. On the plane, he told himself he'd been right—no messy scene, no sticky tears. And she'd find another guy quick enough.

But somehow, Sueko had seemed to know, to sense a differentness in their last night together. The inherent instinct of womankind? A thing deep and unlabeled? Brad didn't know. He knew only that her mouth was desperately sweeter, that her body clung to him more sensuously, in a mute plea for its need, tried to bind him closer and inseparably so that he could never, never leave her.

Sueko said nothing out of the ordinary; instead, she fought to hold him with the tiny magnificence of her lovely body, using as weapons her flaring hips, the erectile thrusts of her breasts, the absorbing softness of her thighs. Childwoman, and yet steeped in ancient knowledge. Girlwoman, and yet containing whirlpooling passions that were older than time itself. Sueko—Last Flower.

Damn him; he'd kissed her goodbye in the morning, with the offkey chants of the street peddlers ringing about them, kissed the mobile warmth of her ripe lips and lied. The early freshness was flavored with salt breezes up from Tokyo Bay, brushed with the faint scent of cherry blossoms. And tears clung to her lashes like saddened bits of diamond dew drops. Damn him.

Back in college, with an unsuspected conscience nagging at him, Brad wrote to a friend still in Tokyo, and his apologetic note was passed along to her. That should have ended it, but it didn't. Her letters came back, in the stilted English of a professional letter-writer, never blaming him, accepting his departure with the fatalistic philosophy of her race. And in time, when he didn't answer, her letters stopped coming.

So the episode was closed. There was school, and a growing sense of going nowhere, of not fitting into the cliques and cuteness. A gun hot under his hand, and men cold at his feet had changed Brad Saxon. He took out his frustrations on the gridiron, smashing and battering, but unable to defeat the darkness within himself.

At the end of his sophomore year, the offer came to play pro ball. Brad grabbed it, eager for anything that would lift him out of the infantile campus world. His father didn't like it; there was the traditional position waiting, the obligations to duty and family. Brad didn't say it, but he hadn't thought a hell of a lot about the way the State Department had handled things in Korea, and about how they were fumbling the ball all over the Orient. But he thought those things, and his father finally had to accept his decision to leave college.

Now the world was different—a hard, glittering, moneyed world of body-to-body conflict on the field, of road trips and roaring crowds and newspaper pictures. And the women—dripping furs or youthfully sweatered, but with the same hot light in their eyes, the looks that Roman maidens—and matrons—must have given gladiators fresh from the arena with bloody hands.

A woman in Hollywood, through a chauffeur-delivered note in the dressing room—a note expensively scented and wrapped around a hundred dollar bill. An apartment in stark blacks and whites, throbbing music from a hidden hi-fi; champagne and a firmly modeled body stripped and pulsating for him. No, Brad thought—not for *him*, but for the brute force he represented. And he was brutal for her, bruising

53

the paleness of her taut thighs, crushing the soft rose-buds of her breasts, hurting her avid mouth with his own.

It hadn't been love-making, but closer to hate-making; the woman needed to be soiled, to be conquered, and he was the savage she had chosen to defeat her. His mouth tasted of stale champagne and secondhand lipstick when he left her, when he took his gladiator's hard body away from her and went angrily into the night. There were other notes from her, but he sent them back unopened. For there were always other women—the young ones all starry-eyed; the older ones trying to hire a stud. Some he took. Some he avoided. None had the touch of a little Japanese girl.

So the darkness remained inside him, a lumped and constant thing. It made Brad a hell of a tackle, always driving, always merciless, more than willing to take his lumps—seeking bruises and hurt as a subconscious gesture toward punishment. Stubbornly, he wouldn't admit the things gnawing at him. Until the bad knee brought it out; until he had the time and money that enabled him to admit it.

In every club in the league, Brad Saxon was known as a hard-headed, mulish guy who'd keep getting up and coming in, no matter how hard he was hit, no matter if cleats and elbows and sly fists were used on him. That trait didn't change when he made up his mind to come back to Japan and find the girl he'd left.

Squealing brakes lurched him toward the driver's seat. Brad came back to himself with a jolt.

"This drug store, sir," the driver said.

Brad unfolded his legs and crawled out of the cab to pay the man. When the taxi pulled away, he stood for a moment looking at the garishly lighted arch of Yokohama's main shopping center—Ize Zaki Cho. All glitter and bustle, all hurrying bright kimonos and business suits; the wooden rattle of foot-slapping *geta* mingled with the rubbered tread of GI boots and the whispering sighs of holiday *zori*. Girls laughed; shopkeepers chanted; GIs shouldered through the crowd.

Recalling spur-of-the-moment shopping sprees with Sueko, Brad turned away. They'd had so much fun, doing silly things—browsing among piled merchandise in miniature shops, buying ridiculous gadgets, arguing with merchants over the price of octopus and black mushrooms.

Brad looked at the grimy windows of Yokohama's leading Sex Drug Store. Someone moved beyond them. Brad went inside, nostrils flaring at strange, unrecognizable scents, eyes flicking from one displayed object to another. There were things here he'd never seen before—tools and cunning imitations only whispered about in the States. And a squat, chunky man in a tight white coat smirking at him across a fly-specked counter.

Brad was direct. "I'm looking for someone—Miss Kamiya Sueko. I was told to try this place."

Sliding over him, the man's eyes marked everything, Brad's size and strength, the tailored suit, the stubborn set of his jaw. Brad stared back, seeing a Japanese bigger than average, with a too-wise mouth and ropily muscled shoulders.

"Well?"

The man rubbed his hands together. "You pay?"

"Damned right I'll pay."

"Maybe not cheap."

Brad took a deep breath. "Listen, buster—I said I'd pay, and I don't care how much it costs, if you can take me to Sueko. But if you try to kid me—"

Big hands braced on the heavy counter, Brad's arms creaked. The massive wood and marble construction tilted and dropped back. The Japanese got the idea.

"Wait," he said, and trotted to the front of the store to click off lights and lock the door. Then he motioned to Brad. "This way. In back. You see."

Just like that. He'd see Sueko in just a moment, and all the mistakes, all the lonely years would be wiped away as if they'd never existed. Mouth dry, Brad followed the man past other counters, through a corridor lined with packing crates. The Japanese paused at another door, rapped on its thick panels with spaced knocks. What the hell, Brad wondered. More mystery. Then he remembered things Mr. Hara said, the warnings of Johnny Kojima that Sueko might be mixed up in businesses she couldn't get out of. Well, he'd see about that.

The door swung back and Brad stooped inside it. There was no warning, no flurry of motion that he could detect before something metal crushed viciously across his neck and drove him to his knees.

Dimly, he heard a whinnying laugh, the scuff of several pairs of feet across the concrete floor. And the slam of a heavy bolt across the door behind him. Brad pushed at the floor, shook his head and felt pain blaze up from the back of his neck.

Somebody laughed again, and a straw-sandaled foot kicked him in the mouth. That was a mistake. Brad clamped steel fingers around an ankle and jerked. Head rocking, he crawled atop the man as he hit the floor, and pounded at his face. There were others on him, hammering, snatching at him. Brad tasted blood, felt blows as numbing shocks without real pain. He struggled up, but they beat him down again. Only not before he got to one of them and dragged the man screaming down with him.

Bright agony lanced thin and swift across Brad's side, but he didn't let go. Big thumbs digging into a rib cage, he tried to tear the man apart like a piece of chicken. Hazily, he remembered locking his teeth into soft flesh and worrying it as a rabid dog might, growling and maddened as men yelled and pounded at him, as they kicked and chopped at him with hard and heavy things. He wouldn't let go. They were killing him, but he wouldn't let go.

Brad never felt the wasp-bite of the needle that punctured his hip, never knew when the mauling and

56

hammering stopped. They had to pry his jaws free of the whimpering Japanese's mangled arm.

"Aiee!" one man cursed. "He is a monster, a tiger. My ribs—"

This one had a twisted leg, and lines of deep bitterness around his mouth.

The bitten man stared at his bleeding arm. Another lay quietly with a pulped face. The muscled one in the white jacket ran exploring fingers over a jaw already swelling with angry welts. "A tiger," he agreed, "but a fat one, also—one whose paws rest in gold."

"I say kill him," Saburo Kamiya spat. "Kill him now."

Kai Watanabe wiped the hypodermic needle on a swab of cotton, shook his head. "Your sister's lover? A man with much money?"

Saburo rubbed his rib cage. "My *sister*—a prostitute, a Yankee plaything!"

"But useful," Kai said. "Very useful, as this man's money will be."

"If you get it. Sometimes I wonder, Kai—which is more important to you, money or the Party."

Kai's face darkened, eyes glittering. "Do not wonder that way again; not aloud. Remember that, or the secret police may find another body in the canal some day. Your sister is useful, Saburo; we can do without *you*."

Flushing, Saburo turned away, dragged his twisted leg to crouch over the unconscious Brad Saxon. Kai put the hypo back into a leather kit, pointed at the bitten man. "Bind that up, then get the truck. The Yankee will lie quietly for a long time."

Saburo glanced up. "Back to Tokyo?"

"Yes. He will be safe in one of my business houses there. After he is put away, you will return home—in case your sister comes to visit. And Saburo—don't let your bitterness make you say anything. You wouldn't look nice in the canal."

57

Saburo chewed his lips. "I wouldn't tell her anything. Sueko still thinks she—*loves*—this one. Love!"

"A commodity," Kai murmured as he brought ropes to tie Brad's hands and feet, "a very profitable commodity."

It was, in his legendary House of All Nations in Tokyo. Kai Watanabe had capitalized on physical love, built it into a thriving business by catering to the craving for infinite variety most men felt. Kai's prices were high, deliberately so. They kept out average American soldiers with only a few Yen to spend, but lured high-ranking officers and rich businessmen who thought cost and quality were the same words.

In the plush, discreet confines of the House of All Nations, this Brad Saxon could be hidden easily, and held there—perhaps as a more or less willing guest—until messages and money could cross the ocean. Kai nodded, very pleased with himself. A shrewd man could always find a method to turn a profit while doing the Party's bidding. The council didn't have to know anything about this little operation. Their orders had been carried out. Get the American. Keep him away from Sueko Kamiya before he causes trouble.

Kai had done that. There he was, trussed like a pig and being loaded into an innocent delivery van. Who was to say that Kai shouldn't hold the American for a tidy ransom—say about ten thousand dollars worth? In green money of course. That would triple itself by crossing into China.

Such dealings might take time, naturally, and the method? Kai smiled. The Party was thorough, painstaking in their searches of background and family. As they'd done with Sueko Kamiya, learning the pressures that could be put upon her, learning the weak and tender spots that could be used to force her to do what they wished.

And as they'd done with this big Yankee. With a father in the US State Department, it shouldn't be too difficult to smuggle ten thousand American dollars into Japan—perhaps in a diplomatic briefcase immune from customs search. Kai's smile widened. Even foreign diplomats were helping Kai Watanabe to become the biggest man in Japan.

"Ready," Saburo said, and Kai nodded to the driver, then waited until the van pulled out of the back alley before going back into his storeroom. A quick phone conversation brought the usual clerks back to duty. Kai didn't want to leave the store closed too long. That meant a drop in profits.

Snug in his American Buick, Kai gave his chauffeur orders and leaned back. He napped along the way, smiling in his sleep.

CHAPTER VIII

The man was sitting at the end of the bed. He had a pistol pointed at Brad, a bluesteel gun with a ridged silencer on the end of its barrel. He had a drooping mouth and blackember eyes.

Brad's mouth creaked open; there was dark fuzz in the back of his throat. His eyes seemed glued. He ached all over, as if the whole damned forward wall of the Los Angeles Rams had run over him. Brad looked at the gunman again. The guy was familiar, but Brad's head hurt. The glue stuck his eyes together, blurred them.

Water splashed into his face, dribbled down to his bare chest, slid off to dampen the sheet. It felt good. Brad opened his mouth to lick its coolness from his lips. When he looked again, there were two men, and he knew them both.

"A word of warning," Kai Watanabe said. "You will be quickly shot if you cause trouble. Saburo has volunteered to guard you, and he would enjoy pulling that trigger."

Brad struggled to sit up, fell back limply.

"That will wear off," Kai continued. "Remember that Saburo hates you, and all Americans, for crippling him. I should be sorry to lose the money, too."

"M-money?" Brad's words were clumsy because his tongue was so thick.

Kai explained about the ransom, concisely and to the point. A letter to Brad's father in Washington, one that would demand an answer within three days. The money to arrive in a courier pouch, an airtight plan.

"But," Kai said, "we will give you time to rest and clear your head, time to think. And one more thing, Saxon-*san*—if you have any heroic ideas, forget them. You came here to find Sueko. You'll be of no use to her as a corpse."

"Damn you," Brad grunted, and made it to a sitting position this time. "Where is she?"

"In due time," Kai said, "in due time. Meanwhile, feel free to enjoy yourself. This is the place for it."

"The hell with you." Brad said. "No letter, no ransom. Hell with you."

Saburo started forward, gun raised. Kai put out a hand. "Consider, Saxon-*san*. It would be a shame to die before you found your love."

Trip-hammers were going inside Brad's head. "You'll have to prove she's alive."

Smiling, Kai shrugged. Brad noticed he wasn't wearing the white jacket now, but good Hong Kong tweeds. "She's alive," he said.

"Prove it. Bring her to me."

"Sorry. You would disrupt Sueko's—assignment. But perhaps her voice—a recent photo?"

Brad rubbed his forehead; he was feeling stronger, the strange lethargy was fading from the body. "Pictures can be faked; voices, too."

Saburo spat. "Let me *make* him write the letter."

Kai raised an eyebrow. "I don't think you could. Saxon-*san*—what proof would you demand?"

"I want to *see* her."

Kai considered. "Tonight, then."

"What?" Saburo shouted in Japanese. "You would bring Sueko here—allow her to meet this—"

"Shut up," Kai ordered. "He will see her; she will not see *him*. We will use the special room—the one with the mirror that is a window. He can watch from hiding."

"Well?" Brad said.

"Tonight," Kai agreed. "With Saburo's gun at your head."

Brad sank back upon the bed.

If they'd send him food and something to drink, he'd be all right soon. And if they brought Sueko here, her brother might get that pistol shoved down his throat.

They fed him well, and even topped off the meal with good Scotch. Kai seemed to get a kick out of treating Brad as an honored guest, although Saburo sulked and muttered from his corner. The gunman stood in the open door as Brad showered in the bath, wincing at the shallow knife gash along his ribs, at the collection of blue areas dotting his body. He'd been worked over pretty good in the drug store, but that wouldn't slow him up any, when he decided to move. But he couldn't try anything until they brought Sueko to him.

Kai hadn't been secretive about where he was being held, and Brad thought the House of All Nations was as good a place as any to hide a guy. From what he'd heard, a lot of men would give their right arms to be hidden here, from now on. Every man who came through the Far East talked about the place; its fame was legendary. But only a select few ever got through the front door, even if they brought AWOL bags full of Yen. The House of All Nations was special, and selected its clients that way.

It was what the name implied—a luxurious house of prostitution stocked with women from many countries, an establishment where a man could pick the color of skin and hair and eyes, where he could choose from svelte, lush offerings brought from around the world. It was a big-money operation, and a clearinghouse for other things beside passion. Clientele of the House of All Nations possessed bits of information that often dropped from careless lips—bits and dribbles that could be woven into an understandable chart of activities of the American Army in Japan and Korea, plaited into a tapestry that predicted future diplomatic maneuverings.

And the burly, oily-smiling Kai seemed to be the king pin. Brad slipped back into his wrinkled clothing and thought that the man had a character trait common to a lot of men—money-hunger. It just might cause him to hang himself.

But Kai was smart enough not to give him half a chance to make a break. He was tied firmly to a heavy chair in the room behind the two-way mirror, far ahead of the time Sueko was supposed to arrive. Saburo stood close behind him, the silenced gun pressed against Brad's neck.

Forced to it or not, Brad had a ringside seat at the damnedest beauty parade he'd ever seen. It was actually staged for the plump, bored Oriental businessman seated on a low leather couch in the next room, but Brad Saxon was in on it, too—and a helluva lot more interested. A hidden loudspeaker announced each girl's name as she appeared at one doorway and crossed slowly and pirouetting to the other.

"This is Sophia," the box announced, as the tall, leggy blonde in a black negligee entered, "a White Russian born in China; she came to Japan after the war."

The thin, lacy material Sophia wore snugged her here and billowed there, hiding very little. She walked as if she'd been oiled at all the proper places, undulating and brazen. She smiled, whirled to expose a gleam of tapering legs, and drifted out of the room, her honey-colored hair swaying almost to her hips.

Mara came in next, dark, bubbling, and Portuguese —and all of eighteen years old. She was a rounded whirlwind with teasing black eyes, vital and alive, skipping across the room.

"Nala," the loudspeaker said. "Arabian; she traveled here from Algeria."

Sloe-eyed Nala's raven hair clustered in tight ringlets on her slim, tanned neck. She wore a simple white *sari*, drawn tightly to outline each curve, and although Nala was willowy, there was plenty to outline.

Brad swallowed at the sight of auburn Francine, whose Old World petiteness and short, frankly feminine nightie bore the stamp of Paris.

Brad had barely recovered from Francine when it was Alice's turn. She was an Englishwoman, red-haired and plump. Not pudgy, but full-thighed and high-breasted with a translucent skin stretched tightly over firm flesh that threatened to burst out of it. Alice, Brad thought, would make quite an armful.

But N'Gere was a proud, six foot tall woman who wore only a golden cloth draped across her hips, and dangling golden earrings to match. Her velvety skin glowed with a black fire, and Brad could hear jungle drums and smell palm oil when she swung past, her erect, muscled body regally savage.

Then T'sao pattered in, and he felt there should be incense, and the sounds of silvered gongs in the distance, for her tiny body brought with it all the silken mystery of forgotten Mandarins. So like Sueko, Brad thought—so very much like Sueko.

He didn't catch the next girl's name, remembering only that it was something melodious. She was high-cheekboned, her eyes slightly oblique, with a polished ivory body that combined the best feature of both East and West. She was Eurasian, and a maddening beauty.

The final woman to make the slow, tantalizing parade was American as mid-western beer, deep-breasted, wide-hipped, with palebrown hair coiled neatly around her shapely head. Brad stared at the white shorts that displayed solid thighs, at the strained halter knotted about her thrusting breasts. A Junoesque woman, rich-mouthed and sultry; no youngster, but an experienced, knowing woman. She was tanned, strong, and had tiny lines of something about her red lips. Cynicism? Self-hate? Brad couldn't tell.

The watching customer sat erect on his couch as she postured for him, as she put both hands behind her head and pushed her breasts into bold relief, as she spun to show the entrancing sweep of her back and haunches. The man struck a brass gong with a little hammer. He'd made his choice.

Beth was her name, and she moved to meet the customer, stood tall and still before him as he ran eager hands over her. Brad turned his head, felt the cold mouth of the pistol thrust into his neck.

"Pull the curtain," he said. "I'm not anxious to see this."

"Be quiet," Saburo hissed. "Does it turn your stomach to watch one of *your* women taken by a Japanese? Does it hurt a Caucasian's pride? You don't think of that when you take *our* women, Yankee. Watch it!"

The pistol forced Brad's head to the front. He caught a glimpse of Beth dropping the bandanna from the fullness of her breasts, saw her lift one slow, gleaming leg at a time to step out of her white shorts. Then he closed his eyes. Saburo could prod all he wanted to, with that damned gun. He wasn't going to look.

Not that he gave a damn who did what to whom; it was their business. He just didn't get his kicks from watching, although he supposed the oily Kai was well paid for this seat in the room behind the mirror. Brad couldn't close his ears. He heard the flesh-on-flesh noises, the quickdrawn, sobbing breaths of the woman in the other room, a rhythm that mounted to a moaning crescendo. He also heard Saburo's panting, the delighted hissing of his guard's excitement.

When it was over, he watched the now-empty room through slitted eyelids. If Kai wasn't bluffing, soon Sueko would come through that door. Then nobody on earth could make him close his eyes again.

65

Sueko, whose utter loveliness was a special, jeweled thing. All the women who'd marched sinuously through that room had been beautiful, but they lacked something that was an intregal part of Sueko. She had an inner radiance, a sublime glow that suffused her adorable body. It set her apart from all other women. At least for Brad Saxon.

The far door opened. Moving daintily, walking with fluid grace, Sueko Kamiya entered the room, and back into his life.

CHAPTER IX

It was no trick, no elaborate hoax set up to deceive him. Brad stared through the false mirror into the other room. Ropes cut into his ankles and wrists as his muscles tensed. There was no doubt about it— the woman was Sueko.

With a walk like music, she reached the center of the room and stopped, hesitating, puzzled. Brad caught his breath. She was older, of course, but the years had been more than kind to Sueko, fulfilling the promises her youth had made, spreading the bud of her loveliness to a full and radiant flower.

Her hair had its own dark glow, a waterfall of soft curls flowing down to caress the small of her back. Her face turned to him, still holding in its maturity some of the little girl quality that was a part of Sueko. And there was sadness in it, a sorrow imbedded behind her eyes, into the bruised flower of her mouth.

"Sueko!"

Saburo ground the gun muzzle into his neck. "She cannot hear you, fool. This room is soundproof."

From the door Sueko had come through, Kai Watanabe drifted in. Smiling, he took her arm, said something that Brad couldn't make out, and led her over to stand close to the mirror. Brad tensed, for he could almost touch the sadness in her eyes, almost smell the musky scent of her perfume.

Maybe it was all in Brad's imagination, but he thought he saw a shadow cross her face, a strange stirring that told him she sensed something out of the ordinary, something almost forgotten that had returned. Damply red, her lips parted. A pulse throbbed in the ivory column of her throat. It was too much.

Brad planted his feet solidly against the floor, leaned·forward into his bonds, then heaved back, shoving up with all the power in his knotted legs. The big chair and two hundred thirty pounds of angry man hurtled backward and smashed Saburo into the wall.

Fighting against the ropes, Brad rolled himself and the chair over, wedged the top against one wall, angled his feet across the corner and got leverage. His shoulders bulged; cords stood out in his throat; veins swelled in his temples. Creaking, the ropes drew tauter, stretching, cutting into his wrists. Wood splintered, snapped. The chair fell apart in an explosion of splinters. Brad stood up, kicked free of the wreckage around his legs, snatched at ropes trailing loose from his arms.

He spun, drove himself at the stunned Saburo as the gun went off with a flat and spiteful cough. Something vicious slapped past Brad's ear. His lifted knee crashed into Saburo's head, slammed it back. The gun skidded across the room. Brad whirled around, heard sounds from the other room—a startled scream, a man cursing in guttural Japanese.

Then he saw the reason he could hear them—the spiderwebbed bullet hole punched neatly through the glass. He caught a flash of Sueko's face, her mouth wide, before she was yanked away from the broken mirror. Brad crouched, tucked in his chin and shielded his face with crossed forearms. He threw himself at the glass, legs pistoning in the power that had made him the terror of opposing linemen across the nation.

He went through the glass like a maddened hurricane, showered it glittering into the room as he dove, landed sprawled on his hands and knees in a thousand shards. He was up in a split second, lunging up and out with his hands spread wide.

But he was too late. The hem of Sueko's dress flashed as she was dragged through the door. Brad hurled himself at the wood, bounced off, gathered his weight again and tore it from its hinges on the second try. The next room was empty. Hoarse-voiced, he shouted it: "Sueko! Sueko!"

Only an echo answered him. Brad snatched open another door, peered wildly into a deserted hallway. He ran to another. Locked. He kicked in the panels. Another empty hall. "Sueko!"

A tuxedoed man darted into the hall, waving both hands at Brad. Brad caught him at the belt line, threw him across the room. Damn Kai; he'd snatched Sueko away from him. He'd kill the grinning ape. Nobody could stop him from getting to Sueko. Nobody.

Brad raged down one hall after another, battering doors down, smashing furniture that stood in his way. He bellowed Sueko's name over and over. Men struck at him, came in pairs and trios to try and bear him down. He crushed them, snarling through the red haze that clotted his eyes, used piledriver fists and big cruel feet, used his weight and the top of his head and his shoulders.

An elbow into this yelling; another room to crash into. A knee driving the wind of some little man with a blackjack; a couch to be ripped apart when he found it empty. Women screaming, their shrieks mingling with the berserk thunder in his ears.

He lifted a bed, speared it through a double window, and paused, growling deep in his throat. A whistle shrilled in the distance; men shouted. Someone tugged at his sweaty arms, and he spun on his heel to tear the man to bits. It wasn't a man.

White-faced, Beth shouted at him. "Come on—run! You can't fight the whole police force. Run, mister!"

He blinked down at her. This was the strong, arrogant woman with the full, pulsing body he'd seen in the parade—the American. She still wore the white shorts and halter. "Hurry!" she insisted, and pulled at him.

The fever began to fade in him. Sueko was gone from this house, spirited away by the oily Kai. But he'd find her again. Somewhere, somehow, he'd find her again.

Beth pulled at him, and he stumbled after her through a dark corridor with the sounds growing louder behind them. Then they were into the coolness of the night. Panting, the woman led him to a car, pushed him into it, then whipped around to the driver's side. She threw the car out of the back alley like a popped champagne cork, rocked it with protesting tires around corners, and straightened it out with a lurch on the open road. Nightwind roared into the open windows, cooling the sweat on Brad's face, dampening the flames within.

Damn; he hadn't been so mad in a long time. Not since that nest of Reds on Hill 609 pinned the outfit down. After Mike Connors got it beside him, something snapped in Brad. When the yelling stopped and the smoke cleared, he'd been standing spreadlegged among four dead men in what was left of the gun position. They told him he'd used the blistering gun itself to hammer down the last Red, searing his hands.

Brad rubbed his face. Going wild that way didn't help him now, though. Sure, he'd wrecked the House of All Nations—but that didn't bring Sueko to him. Now the cops would be after him in force. Brad dropped his hand. If Mr. Hara didn't keep them off his back. Hara. The little guy was going to be mad as hell about Brad going down to Yokohama, after he'd told Brad to stay put.

But maybe he'd stirred up something. At least, now he knew a couple of names, some starting places they could fan out from. Sueko's image stayed with Brad—sweet, bewildered. She didn't look like the girl people

70

were hinting she was; she looked as beautiful as ever; even more so. He remembered how she'd been dressed--a clinging, silken dress, impeccably tailored; sheer nylons cupping the swell of her tapering calves; high heels; a sparkle of jewelry at her throat, on her hand.

Brad clenched his fists. Expensive clothing; diamonds. Where would a girl like Sueko get diamonds? Not from customers of any house of prostitution in Japan—not even the exclusive House of All Nations; profit didn't go to the girls, but into the pockets of slobs like Kai Watanabe.

He looked at Beth's face, tense and ghostly in the glow from the dash lights. "You can drop me anywhere along here."

She didn't turn, but eased up on the gas pedal. "And let the cops pick you up before you get two blocks?"

"Why did you help me back there? You don't know me, don't know why I was taking the place apart."

Beth turned the car into the Yokohama cutoff. "You're American, and maybe—well, maybe you were doing something I'd wanted to do, myself."

Brad sat quietly for awhile. It was none of his business why she was working in a house like that. This car, her obvious education and poise didn't point toward a need for money. What, then? Nymphomania, a restless, never-sated sexual drive?

"I know what you're thinking," she said. "And Beth Buckley isn't the only Army wife on call at the House of All Nations. Of course, that's no excuse, and I'm not looking for any. I knew what I was doing when I went there the first time. After that—well—it wasn't so easy to get out."

Kai Watanabe, Brad thought. Cunning and greedy, Kai would never allow an attractive piece of merchandise like Beth to slip through his hungry fingers. Once on the inside, she'd have to stay there, like it or not. She'd said something about Army wives. Blackmail could be the club Kai held over Beth, and over other women like her.

"Where are we going?" Brad asked.

She chuckled, but it wasn't a happy sound. "To my quarters, or rather to the quarters of Colonel Jeremy H. Buckley—Jerry, to his friends. Although at the moment, I can't think of any friends he has."

Brad started to say something, but she moved one hand from the steering wheel and squeezed his arm. "Please. I'd like to know why you were in such a magnificent rage; maybe I can help. And I'm being a little selfish, too. I'm—I'm frightened."

The night flowed by, dotted with occasional pools of yellow light, spiced with farm country odors, broken by bell noises. Brad decided why not? Sueko was hidden away somewhere by now, the Tokyo police were in an uproar, and probably had men waiting at his hotel. Kai would be more than upset at the damage to his place, and Saburo's hate would be dangerous as he nursed his broken face. Brad found it difficult to think of Saburo as Sueko's brother; more than his leg was warped and twisted. Yet he *was* the girl's blood kin. Brad certainly wasn't building up many points on his side. Sueko might hate him for what he'd done.

Beth braked the car in front of a big house. Brad looked for a guarded gate, didn't find it. "Special quarters," Beth explained. "The colonel feels he has to be close to the people." She sounded as if she was about to cry. "If—if you'll wait in the car a minute, I'll talk to the maid. I'm sure we can use her rooms out back."

She was gone. Brad listened to faint night sounds around him, and wondered about Beth Buckley. His first impression of her had been correct; she was no schoolgirl. He'd judge her age at about thirty-three to thirty-five. It was difficult to tell. Maybe under a strong, harsh light, there'd be a network of fine lines about her eyes and mouth, a slight sagging of the flesh

72

under her chin. But back in the house, and beside him in the car, she'd looked fine; real fine. Brad thought that Colonel Buckley must be a damned fool.

A shadow came across the lawn, feminine even in the dark. "Okay," she said. "Eimiko was a little shocked, but she is used to the strange ways of foreigners. Follow me around, and don't worry—the colonel isn't home. He rarely is."

The maid's quarters were separate from the big house, warm and cozy, and a mixture of both the Orient and the West. The bed was Japanese, though, silken *futons* folded upon straw *tatami* mats, with the usual cylindrical pillow.

Beth brought a hand from behind her, displayed a bottle. "I rescued this from the house. It's all right to go—go native, but I can't stand their—their *sake*—"

Her face crumbled around the edges; her eyes blurred. Abruptly, she sat down upon the *futon* and covered her eyes. Beth's voice was muffled. "I—I'm sorry; delayed reaction, I guess. I'll be all right in a moment."

Brad took the bottle, looked around and found a pair of porcelain rice bowls; they'd do. He poured whisky into them, offered Beth one when she looked up. She downed it at a gulp and held the bowl out for a refill. She only drank half of this one.

"I already know your name," Brad said. "Mine's Brad Saxon; nothing in front of it."

Beth dabbed at her eyes. "Department of the Army Civilian?"

He shook his head. "A DAC? Not me. Just a foot-loose guy who doesn't work for anybody."

She tried to smile. "Tourists don't often find the House of All Nations."

"No tourist, either. I came back to find somebody."

"A girl," Beth said. "I heard you roaring her name."

Brad stared at her. "Sueko. Does—does she work there?"

73

"No, I don't think so. I never heard of any Japanese girls there."

Her eyes were threatening to spill over again, so Brad poured her another drink. "She was there—just for a minute. Kai had me wrapped up in the room behind the mirror. I broke out, but she was gone."

Beth swallowed, turned her face. "Then you—you saw me with that—"

"You don't owe me any explanation," Brad said. "I figure people do what they have to."

"Brad—"

"My drink's getting warm," he said, and tossed it off.

"I'd like to tell you—"

"You don't have to," Brad said.

"I know that, but didn't somebody say confession was good for the soul, or something?"

Brad saw the quick drinks she'd absorbed were taking hold, mixing with the emotional letdown of the getaway she'd helped him make. Beth's cheeks were flushed, her mouth looser now, and dewy. In this light, she had the lines around her eyes. In other circumstances, they might have been the tracks of laughter.

Beth finished her drink, shoved the bowl out for more. "I—I went to that—place in Tokyo for spite, I guess. As a way of striking back at my husband. He—he's been keeping a Japanese mistress for almost a year. I tried to make him give her up. He wouldn't. He offered me a divorce, but I wouldn't. You can't imagine how—how it hurts a woman's pride to be replaced so casually. Call it feminine illogic, anything —but I wanted to hurt him, as he hurt me, to punish him by offering my—my body to anyone who'd pay for it."

She swallowed, stared at the colorful patterns worked into the *futon*. "I guess I might as well be perfectly honest, while I'm at it. Jerry—I—well, dammit, I'm human, too. I need love as much as any man

74

does. And when he—when my husband didn't—didn't want me any more, I—"

Brad hushed her by placing fingertips gently against her mouth. "Okay; that's enough."

Beth's eyes matched her lightbrown hair; they moved up along his corded arm and locked into his own, something besides the liquor stirring in them. Brad withdrew his hand. She caught at it, held it as she slid forward and lifted her lips. They were spicy, warmsweet with whisky, mobile against his mouth. Slowly, he pulled back from her and picked up his bowl again.

"You—I guess I don't blame you," she said huskily. "You wouldn't want a—a woman who's been had by so many men, a d-dirty woman—"

"That's not it," Brad said.

She was still very close, her bare knee touching his leg, her soft hand on his arm. "The girl, then? The one you came back for?"

Brad nodded. "That's part of it, I guess. And maybe it's because you're still just trying to strike back at your husband."

Beth trembled; he felt the shudders rake her. "Please, Brad. You—you must love her very much. Please share just a tiny bit of that love with me. I—I need to be loved, *really* loved, even if only for a little while. If you don't—don't mind what I am—"

This time, he cut off her words with his lips, searching gently into her open mouth, trying to still her fears, calm the self-hate, to show her she was a desirable woman, no matter what she had done.

Beth moulded the electrifying length of her long, rounded body to him, clinging with a desperation that soothed slowly into deepening need. Firm, jutting breasts flattened against his chest; her writhing torso began a sensuous tick-tocking. Beth's white shorts slipped away easily in his hands; the halter seemed to vanish of its own accord.

Sliding flesh, vibrant flesh moved to him, with him

75

in a growing frenzy. Her scented skin was the texture and feel of new satin, tingling, downy. Beth's hands caught at his head, locked around his head as she lifted squirming to him. He was strong with her, and gentle with her, blending his own hungers with hers, master and yet being mastered.

They were good for each other. He was her need, her justification, the numbing of her conscience. And she was a softstring and loving woman, crying out in her loneliness to him, to his maleness. The magic of their entwined bodies swelled, seethed in gentle fury, swirled toward the enchanted point where it would boil blazing forth and dissolve them.

"Tell me," Beth gasped into his throat. "Tell me you love me—please, Brad, tell—me—you—love—me."

A series of rippling spasms shook her body, clenched her straining thighs. Her bared teeth worked over his collarbone, into the flat muscle of his chest. "Brad—Brad—Brad—"

"I love you," he said into the woman scent of her coiled braids, into the violence and prayer of her. "I love you, Beth."

And he did, at that moment, when the cresting swept to a new and impossible height, when the foaming waves shuddered and bubbled and raced quivering down a faraway flume. At that moment, he loved Beth Buckley, because she was Beth, and Sueko, and all women past, all women to come. Because she, for that one brightgleam fragment of time, loved him also.

They slid together into a pool of warm relaxation, held softly to each other until she began to cry—not with body-wracking sobs, but easily, as if a barrier had been broken, and a long-pent flood released. Brad let her cry it out, cuddled her and petted her as he would a hurt child.

In time, she pulled away from him, keeping her face turned as she fumbled for the shorts and halter. When her clothing was adjusted, she looked at Brad.

"Thank you," she said. "Thank you, Brad Saxon—for what you are, and for what you've shown me I can be."

He had no answer for her, none that wouldn't sound stiff and rehearsed, so he lifted the limp fingers of her pale hand and kissed them.

"Will-will you stay here tonight?" she asked. "With me? Can you—can you pretend for tonight that I'm your Japanese girl? Then I'll help you find her again, help you any way I possibly can."

Brad smiled, touched her shining hair. "Of course I'll stay, and I won't pretend you're anyone but yourself. You're a wonderful woman, Beth—a woman who'd honor any man by her love."

Much later, Brad would remember saying that to her. Because Beth Buckley would be more important to him than either of them dreamed.

CHAPTER X

Somewhere out on the Bay, a hoarse metallic voice warned ships away from rocks shrouded by gathering fog. On the street outside the maid's house, a late taxi scurried muttering to its den. The city slept.

Beth Buckley drew on her cigaret, watched the red glow brighten, then fade. She lay on her back, one satin knee drawn up, conscious of the coolness of night air on her nude body. Listening, she heard the man stretched beside her breathing—deep and comforting sounds.

She couldn't sleep; she didn't want to sleep. She wanted to lie quietly and remember the man. As if she could forget him. Ruefully, Beth made a bitter smile into the darkness. So this was what it was really like—this melting and mingling together, one with the other, enmeshed in the hardwarm strength of him, giving and taking while the world trembled and time paused breathless in its flight.

It had almost been like that before; almost. And too many years ago. Orange blossoms and white lace under the traditional crossed sabers; bells and the laughing scamper through showering rice to the car. Jerry—without the creases in his neck, without the swollen belly and more swollen ego—Jerry rigid and penetrating, sweetpain and glad release of healthy lust.

Beth pulled on the cigaret. Smoke didn't taste right, when you couldn't see it. When, she wondered, had the change taken place? Could she point back through the years and say: here—right here is when it happened? She didn't think so. The change was insidious, creeping, feeding upon itself through time and the exchange of metal designs upon collars— Jerry's collars. Maybe all husbands grew away from their wives like that; Beth didn't know.

Parties became important, and important people became vital; so had prestige and status and sly back-stabbing to get what you wanted. The quick, sudden gusts of passions had faded, paled into a mechanical habit. But where was the mellowing, the deepening togetherness that was supposed to come with time?

Beth wouldn't have minded the death of romance in her marriage, if something else had replaced it. Nothing had. Only arrogance and sarcasm and emotions closely akin to hate. Being transferred to Japan had really finished whatever she and Jerry Buckley had once had between them.

Maybe she was strait-laced, old-fashioned in the fullest sense of the phrase, because she hadn't succumbed to the coy approaches of her husband's friends and fellow officers at cocktail parties. Beth hadn't gone in for the sweaty pawing on back porches, for whisky-wet kisses snatched in hallways. Not even when she saw Jerry doing the same—and worse.

But when the colonel found his new, and evidently hypnotically attractive mistress, it was time to do something. She couldn't sit home alone every night while he sported with his Oriental concubine. And Beth couldn't bring herself to make a play for any of the men she knew. She drank, numbing her loneliness early in the day, sleeping sodden through the nights. That didn't work, either.

She tried to bring matters to a head by confronting Jerry, by demanding that he give up his mistress and keep their marriage intact. It was too late. He was too firmly entrenched in his position, knew too many people, had too many favors owed him for a divorce to hurt him in military circles.

79

He'd laughed at her. "Your jealousy is showing, darling. Give up my mistress? Never. But I won't stand in the way of a divorce for you."

Beth saw he actually wanted that, wanted a divorce. "No," she said, "Damn you—no!"

Jerry lifted fat shoulders. "You'll pardon me, my dear? I'm late for an appointment."

Just like that. Take it and like it, or go home and call it quits. She'd be damned if she would. She'd married him for better or for worse, and that rule applied to both of them. All right, then. She'd find a way to strike back.

She did, since Japan is full of semi-deserted wives who, knowing or unknowing, share their husbands with Japanese girls. A word here, a bit of gossip there, and Beth Buckley got her inspiration. Everybody had heard of the infamous House of All Nations, where women of many countries were for hire. Helped by nearly a fifth of bourbon, Beth stalked into the place and asked for a job before she lost her courage.

Kai Watanabe had been unctuous, bowing and smiling at her. And she'd joined the parade of beauties that very night, a little frightened, but determined to go through with it. Beth didn't know what she expected to accomplish. There was some vague idea of smearing her husband by soiling herself. There was also a very real need, a long-unassuaged wanting that screamed silently to be satisfied.

That much, she got. Her first customer was an expert in the arts of physical love, an imaginative man who experimented and teased, who made her initial venture with a man other than her husband a mad and tremendous series of new sensations.

But then there were different kinds of men—weird ones who demanded she do things she had only heard whispered about; savage ones who enjoyed inflicting pain; squirming, sobbing ones who begged her to hurt them. Beth told Kai Watanabe she was quitting, that she had made a mistake.

He jolted her by pulling a folder from his desk drawer. Somehow, he'd gotten her real name and learned everything about her—where she lived, what her husband's job was, even the addresses of her family in the States. He read the information off to her. Then he told Beth to go back to work. She remembered that he had never stopped smiling.

The cigaret seared Beth's fingertips. She felt for an ashtray, ground out the spark. Beside her, the man stirred. Beth lay still. Was he dreaming of the girl—the Sueko he'd roared for in the House of All Nations? What a magnificent, terrifying brute he had been—raging, destroying, flinging men about like twigs. Her first glimpse of him had stopped her in her tracks; those massive shoulders heaving, those great hands literally tearing doors apart in regal fury.

Beth envied a girl named Sueko. What did she have, to make such a man fall in love with her—so much in love that he'd pull down a city to find her? She must be very lovely, Beth thought; and very lucky. Brad Saxon was not only a man's man, he was a woman's man, too. He was a wonderful combination of the things all women wanted—strength and overwhelming male power; and yet so gentle, so understanding. Beth could love such a man.

She frowned into the shadows and thought that perhaps she already did. Dim plans began to form in her mind, vague ideas that were partly fantasies, partly wishes. Brad hadn't told her much—just that he was looking for this Sueko. Suppose he couldn't find her? Suppose she didn't *want* to be found? Wouldn't that make him turn to someone else?

Beth closed her eyes, tried to picture how life would be with Brad Saxon. A man to cling to, a man to honor and obey and to love with every aching fiber of her being. She imagined a somewhere apartment, a huge bed spread with white satin sheets, Brad standing in the shower with water cascading over those chest muscles, purling down his ridged stomach,

81

making rivulets through the crisp curling hairs of his legs. She would be ready on the bed for him, any way he wanted her—in ribbons and laces, or completely nude. Any way he wanted.

He'd come to her with his body still a little damp, smelling of cleanliness and soap, of shaving lotion. And she would hold up her arms to him—

Her hand moved of its own volition, found his back and drew its fingertips along the curve of his spine. Softly, she moved her arm over and around him, turned so that her knees fitted into the hollows of his, moulded her thighs and stomach and breasts to his sleeping body.

Let Kai Watanabe threaten and fume; let him do what he damned well please—expose her for what she had been, a prostitute; he could send the information back to her family, present it to her husband. She no longer cared. Beth had enough of neglect and swinish superiority and mockery. Jerry Buckley wanted a divorce, did he? All right; he could have it. But not until Beth Buckley was good and damned ready to give it to him.

In the meanwhile, she had this man in her arms. She would stay with him and beside him, helping in any way she could—honestly helping, for she already sensed that Brad Saxon was the kind of man everybody *had* to be honest with. Maybe, she thought raggedly, maybe this was the sum and substance of real love—the willingness to bring happiness to the one you loved, no matter what the cost would be to yourself.

She'd help Brad find his Japanese girl. Beth knew a lot of useful people, both military and civilian. She'd go to them, beg their help, even buy it, if she had to. But all the while, she'd be hoping for something to happen, something that would make a difference to Brad. Then she'd be handy, standing by to pick up the pieces.

He moved in her arms, turned slowly to face her on

the *futon,* and she knew he was no longer asleep. Searching through the darkness, her mouth found his and clung. Thrusting, her breasts moved with a life of their own; her hungry hips tried to move impossibly closer.

"Brad," she murmured, "I'm sorry I woke you. I—I didn't mean—"

"Liar," he whispered against her pulsing flesh. "Lovely liar. But I can't think of a better way to wake up."

Neither, she thought as she felt him move, neither could she.

CHAPTER XI

Brad felt slightly uncomfortable sitting in the richly-furnished living room of the colonel's quarters. He could hear the colonel's wife taking a shower, hear the maid rattling breakfast dishes in the kitchen. He held the telephone, listening to buzzing and chirps and quick Japanese voices on the line, while he stared at the gold-framed picture of a man on a nearby table.

If the man who'd posed for that picture came walking through the door now, what would he say to him? Good morning, colonel; thank you for the delightful night I just spent with your lovely and passionate wife? But Beth had said her husband wouldn't be home. Famous last words, Brad thought; just before the shotgun went off.

Still, he had to get himself untracked, get back on the trail of Sueko. Which was why he was calling Lieutenant Johnny Kojima. Not that he wanted to see the CIC agent, but Brad had to find out just how hot the city of Tokyo was for him today. Plus getting in touch with Mr. Hara. Kojima would know how to reach the little man.

The voice was careful; no name-and-rank answer, just a "Yes?"

Brad asked for Kojima, gave his own name.

"Why in hell," Kojima said, "didn't you do that much damage to the Bears?"

Brad grinned. "You mean the House of All Nations?"

"Is there another one missing? Hooboya— certain MP captain is having a stroke."

Brad said: "The drug store lead was pretty good."

"I know from nothing—not over this phone. Meet you somewhere?"

"Can I come to town?"

"Better not," Kojima said. "Know where Ize Zaki Cho is?"

"I ought to."

"The live oyster stand, then. Where tourists dig their own pearls. Clever, these Orientals, eh? Three hours." The phone clicked.

Damn, Brad thought. Kojima had been in such a hurry that there'd been no mention of Mr. Hara. But there'd probably be time for that later. The little guy was no fool; he'd probably connect the riot at the House of All Nations last night with Brad, and start an investigation from there.

Replacing the phone, Brad got up and went over to the framed photo of Colonel Jeremy Buckley. The man had lifted his chin for the photographer, but there were still extra folds of flesh showing. Brad grinned, comparing the man to the legendary "Colonel Blimp" of the British. The resemblance was more than superficial, even if Buckley didn't have the walrus moustache. Small eyes wedged behind pouches that spoke of high living and late hours; a sullenly compressed mouth, flared nostrils.

"Cute, isn't he?"

Beth was wrapped in a fluffy robe, her face clean and shiny.

"I can't help wondering," Brad said.

"Why I married him? 'Something about a soldier,' you know. He used to look good in a uniform. He was ardent, too—a whirlwind romancer, eager to marry me. It took quite awhile before I remembered that my father being an ex-Congressman might have had something to do with it. That can be a help to an ambitious young officer, you know."

85

Brad ran his eyes over her, remembering the textured feel of the statuesque body hidden now by her robe, remembering the wild violence and tenderness of it. "You can do better, Beth. Theres' no reason for a woman like you to stay married to a man she doesn't love. You can find someone who'll appreciate how wonderful you are."

Her own eyes were level, direct. "Can I, Brad?"

"Beth," he said, "You know how I—"

"I'm not crowding you, Brad. I just want you to know that if—if you ever change your mind, I'll be around. And if you can forget what I've done in the past."

"You have no past, only a present—and any future you want to make for yourself."

"Or whatever somebody makes for me," she said, and told him about the dossier Kai Watanabe kept on her. She wasn't worried about it, she added; not now. Not since she'd made up her mind to divorce the colonel. Her family could think what they wanted to; it didn't make much difference.

Brad thought it over. Word had no doubt reached Kai by now that one of his girls was missing. The man would add that information to Brad's escape from the house last night and come up with an answer. Suddenly, Brad felt uneasy. Kai could easily have men outside the Buckley house right now. Or *inside* it.

"Maybe you'd better come with me," he said to Beth. "It might be safer."

"Of course," she said, and turned for her room to dress. "You'll play hell dropping me off this bandwagon." Beth paused, chin over her shoulder. "Not unless you really *want* me off, Brad."

She moved away before he could answer. What the hell *could* he answer, anyway? Could he tell this fine and beautiful woman that he'd never have room in himself for anybody but Sueko, that she'd only bring more hurt and more trouble upon herself if she stayed

86

with him? Not after something to both of them. Maybe too much. What a hell of a world.

Brad forced Beth from his mind momentarily, tried to arrange his thoughts and plan ahead. In less than three hours, he had a date with Johnny Kojima. Perhaps the agent could help, perhaps not. But there was always the Sex Drug Store. That was another place that could stand a thorough working over. If he hurt Kai enough in his tenderest area, his pocketbook, the man would be certain to come looking for him again. And Kai had Sueko.

Unexpected, startling, the scream rang high and terror-filled through the house. Brad flinched, stood frozen for a moment. Beth.

He leaped for the bedroom door, slammed it back with his shoulder. Hunched, snarling, the man whirled from Beth. Brad saw the red print of the man's hand across her throat and lunged in. He hurtled through empty space where the man should have been, and bounced off the wall.

Something chopped him across the neck. Brad spun, reaching. The room turned end over end. He landed hard on his shoulders, breath gusting out in a rush. A shoe heel drove viciously at his throat, and he was barely alert enough to roll dizzily away from it. The second try caught him on the side of the jaw. Lights flashed on and off.

Grunting, he pawed at the floor and came up, shaking his head, trying to brush the red and black spots out of his eyes. The knife edge of a calloused palm lanced into his throat. Brad swayed, sucking through the brighthard agony that wouldn't let the air through. The face before him was out of focus, hazy, leering at him gold-toothed and evil.

Brad stuck a fist at it, felt the hands close around his wrist again. Then they dropped away. Brad spat, forced a gulp of head-clearing air into his chest. The man was on his knees, reaching up to tear a hurricane off his back. Beth Buckley was riding him like a horse, long, gleaming legs locked about his middle, one hand clenched into his short hair, the other raking frantically at his face with clawed fingernails already stained with blood.

Brad wheezed forward, chin pulled in, a red mist dropping over him. He caught the man, got a hand twisted into his coat. Squealing, the Japanese struck at him, but it didn't matter now. As Beth dropped away, the leverage was gone. Brad yanked him off the floor, held him in mid-air and wrapped his other hand around a thin ankle. Then he turned slowly and hammered the man's head against the wall. Plaster cracked. Dust geysered. The man stopped screaming.

Beth wiped her hands on her robe, pulled it together. Her voice was thin and shaky. "He—he was hidden in the closet. My throat—I managed to scream—"

Brad stepped over the inert body, took her in his arms. "You did fine. He'd have ruined me if you hadn't crawled him. That took a lot of nerve, Beth. I guess he's a Judo expert; a clumsy guy like me is a setup for them."

Slowly, Beth stopped shivering. "I—I'm all right now. What—who is he? Do you think Kai sent him?"

Brad stooped over the man, searched his coat. "I don't know. Maybe the guy I have a date with can make something of this wallet." He found something metal in another pocket, brought it out and stared at the deadly little Colt .25. "We're lucky he didn't use this. Guess he thought he could handle me without it."

Beth pressed the back of her hand to her mouth. "Brad—shouldn't we do something? Tell the police?"

He shook his head. "The police aren't very friendly toward me just now, but maybe you ought to call them. Report an attempted burglary, or rape. Did the guy say anything before he jumped you?"

Beth's eyes were wide. "N-no; he just sort of snarled and caught my throat."

"Did you ever see him before? I mean—at the House of All Nations?"

"No; no, I'm sure I haven't. But Kai has so many men working for him—"

Brad slipped the .25 into his own pocket. When he met Johnny Kojima in the shopping center, he'd have to get some more clothes. A couple of more battles, and this suit would fall apart. He looked down at the Judo man. The guy hadn't moved. Frowning, Brad reached inside the man's shirt, kept his hand there awhile. Then he looked up at Beth.

"Better forget about calling the police," he said stiffly. "This guy's not going to answer any questions. He's dead."

CHAPTER XII

Sueko Kamiya was thinking of a man. Moving with small, unconsciously graceful steps through the too-richly furnished living of the big Tokyo house, she thought of Kai Watanabe and his anger. Such anger in such a man was a thing to fear. Never had she seen him so maddened, and she was worried.

It had something to do with Saburo; that much she knew. Kai had muttered things about her brother outliving his usefulness to the *Kyosan-do* . . . the communists. And Kai's rage had something to do with her strange trip to the House of All Nations, and the sudden explosion of a mirror there.

For a moment, she had felt odd, staring into that mirror. As if it were looking back at her; as if she knew the mirror as a friend. No, more than that. As if—

Sueko ran light hands through her hair, shook her head. That was silly. And yet, when Kai ran her out of the room, a man's voice shouting her name. A voice that belonged to the long-dead past, and could not be. A fantasy, a thing so often in her dreams that it seemed real.

Kai Watanabe was no fantasy. He was real and deadly, and held all of her small world in his greedy hands. Saburo—poor, twisted boy who had never grown out of his bitter childhood. Saburo depended upon Kai for everything—a shred of self-respect, a job of sorts, a dim hope for an impossible future. And his very life.

And Katsue, the younger sister who made a household god of money. The tentacles of Kai's organization reached around her, followed her everywhere. They needed only to close, once—and she would be dead. Sueko stood in the center of the big living room, seeing nothing around her. Katsue could not be blamed for following the path her elder sister had taken, for preferring the relatively easy life of the prostitute to the hard and hungry struggles of a shop girl. Perhaps she, too, would learn in time that the easy way was often the most painful.

Could there be any life richer, more protected than Sueko's was now? How many poorly educated girls could claim to be mistress of a house as great as this one, and wear diamonds, and dress in the best imported Western fashions? And how many lived with the grey emptiness that was sucking the life out of Sueko Kamiya?

She tilted her head to one side, stood listening to the old gardener beyond the window carrying on his verbal battle with insects and bad weather. She heard the upstairs maid moving about her tasks, the cook's knife deftly chopping vegetables for tonight's dinner. And the slow plodding of her heart.

Her mother's heart had thumped that way, slower and slower because she willed it so, until at last it stopped. Sueko thought she should feel guilty because she was glad when it happened. But even now, she felt only a sense of relief. At least one of the Kamiya family was beyond reach of Kai Watanabe.

At first, she thought her mother's death might change things, that she could run away. There were still her brother and sister, and in reality, no reason left to run. Sueko remained as the American officer's mistress, stayed on in the big house as a showpiece for his friends, because she was told to; because there wasn't anything else.

And he wasn't a bad man—only sometimes, when he beat her for some fancied wrong. He was loud, and he had soaked himself too long and too thoroughly in strong American whisky, but there were worse men. He was generous, although not even a colonel's pay could support two houses in such luxurious styles. Where the money came from was none of her business. She knew of his other great house in Yokohama, of his wife there. But many American officers had dealings with *yami-chans* . . . the black market heads like Kai Watanabe.

Only this one didn't realize when Kai seemed to be giving, he was really taking, that the colonel's boasts and drunken carelessness were all recorded; that names and incidents and a hundred little stupidities were money in Kai's pockets. Easy money; a matter of small reels of tape from tiny recorders secreted all over the house—bedrooms, baths, everywhere.

It had seemed such a little thing to do for Kai, when he first spoke to her about it. In return for safety of the Kamiyas, all she had to do was send the servants away long enough for the cunning men to install the machines. And twice a week, take out the used reels and replace them with new ones. Then deliver the little spools to Kai. Such a little thing.

Now she knew better. Now Sueko understood how bits and pieces of information were woven into a damaging net that would hurt all Americans. She didn't want all of them hurt. Especially one of them— somewhere. But she wouldn't allow herself to think of him. Instead, she remembered how slyly Kai had groomed her for this job, how he had dressed her and trained her, and gotten her into places where only high-ranking officers gathered to eat and drink and sample Japanese girls.

No more sergeants and corporals for Sueko; no more hectic, gay and sodden "short-times" in the back rooms of the New Opal Hotel. She was special, Kai told her—with a fragile beauty that would appeal to the biggest—and richest—men in Japan. Oh, Kai was devious, and he was shrewd. He'd used the Military Police captain to get her into the right places, to see that she was introduced to the right colonel. Captain Getty had done his job well, and had been well paid for it, too.

And that included the little "bonus" he'd arranged for himself. Sueko shuddered, remembering how the man had come to her room like a great, sweating pig. He was hairy, and reeked of whisky, and was so arrogantly certain of his power. Grunting and rutting upon her, he had snarled when she failed to respond. He had risen at last, finished but not quite satisfied, and spat upon her, telling her that her beauty was a lie. And then he had taken off his belt and left painful stripes across her trembling haunches and the tenderness of her soiled thighs.

She had not cried; she hadn't begged him to stop. She only lay there, mutely hating him until he went away. Sueko knew he would come back, and he did. But the next time, things had changed. She was already the colonel's mistress, already set up in the colonel's house. Smiling coldly, she taunted the big-bellied captain, dared him to touch her. Sueko had hoped he would, so that she could tell the colonel, run sobbing and screaming to the colonel and beg his protection.

Captain Getty's face purpled, and his hairy hands lifted to her, but the pig was more intelligent than he seemed. Choking on his anger, he told her that he would wait, that some day the colonel would tire of her, and then—

But the day had not arrived as yet. Sueko used all the experience she had gained from a hundred men, all the feminine wiles learned from wiser women. She bound the colonel ever tighter to her, held him there with the sensual sweetness of her body, catering to his every whim, anticipating his desires, being anything he wanted her to be. She was a great actress. At times she even came close to fooling herslf. It was easy to imitate, when a woman had once had the real thing.

Sueko sat upon the thick pillows of the Western style couch, felt the silken whispering of nylons as she crossed her knees and reached for a cigaret. She flicked a lighter, tried to force her mind away from the thoughts that crowded in upon it. There was nothing so dead as yesterday. Why then, did the past come creeping unbidden into the present, trailing its grey suns and withered flowers after it like a shroud?

His name was difficult for her to pronounce, at first. So foreign, such hard syllables—Brad. She said it; Brad-u, and he laughed. She liked to hear him laugh, the rumble beginning deep in his broad chest and spreading up and out through the polished brightness of his even teeth. The very first time she heard him laugh, the sound washed away the fear of him, the fright of his great, bearlike size and the obvious strength of many men.

Hai, but he was powerful, with steel in him to match his muscles. And a warborn hate that shouldn't have been part of a man who laughed so well. Sueko remembered that her lipstick had been crudely dabbed on, that the tight foreign dress had seemed ready to split at its seams, and that she had been fearful—not only of her first man, but of making a mistake that would have told the house mama-*san* Sueko was no experienced prostitute, but only a hungry schoolgirl. Tokyo was full of hungry schoolgirls, and the madam required women certain to please the moneyed American soldiers.

Brad came. Alone with his bitterness, carrying his poor, scarred face like a banner, limping across the dance floor to her. He passed the women who spoke better English, who knew how to swing their hips and make their breasts appear higher and fuller. He came directly to her, stood looming over her like one of the massive stone gods in Nikko gardens—so big. He would kill her, she thought with a trembling in her belly. He would lower that tremendous weight upon

94

her, thrusting and tearing until he ripped her apart. She would die.

Sueko wanted to stand up and kick off the wobbly high heels so she could run away from him like the winds of the typhoon. Then he smiled.

"You're a tiny one," he said, "and you're beautiful."

She didn't believe she was beautiful. She was so small. Tiny, he said, and she knew the word from the schoolbooks. Japanese men joked at her because of her smallness, called her baby names. Now this giant foreigner said she was beautiful. He didn't seem to be drunk, although most Americans always were.

As part of her job, Sueko led him to the bar and shared drinks with him. She drank the purplish ice of the wine too quickly, unused to it and turning silly. Yet, when she thought of the room across the courtyard, and its waiting bed, she drank more. Her legs were rubber when she went ahead of him to the room. There had been a moment—one terrifying second, when she almost ran away. But she thought of Saburo's empty stomach and crippled leg, of Katsue scratching lessons on a slate with bluecold fingers, of her mother staring at an empty corner. She didn't run.

She did turn away as he stripped off his shirt. Trembling, she wriggled out of the tight dress and folded it carefully. Hurrying, Sueko slid into the *futon*-covered bed, wondering if it would stand up under the weight of him; if she could breathe under his weight.

He was tender. Big, hard hands turned feathersoft and drifted like spiralling cherry blossoms over her taut and naked body, stroking, caressing. Slowly, she relaxed, hoping that this gentleness would continue, that Brad wouldn't rip and maul her. His hands were everywhere, easy upon her quivering stomach, cupping her aching breasts, working into her hair.

And his mouth, warm-sliding over her cheek, along her throat, softly upon her lips as she lifted to him in the unconscious, inherent motion all women make

95

when they are loved. Brad was not heavy; he was an enfolding shelter, arching over her. Gladly, she offered herself, opening and uncurling.

There was pain, but welcome and sweetswift. There was a small agony of tensed resistance, and then the undeniable piercing, the magic penetration that overcame all fears and all things imagined. Lifting, locking, he blended with her in enchanted movements, in a splendor and hotwild tenderness that melted her, poured her into his flesh and blood. There was a crashing, foaming crest that swept her to the moonsilver sands of a somewhere beach, and left her there limp and unresisting.

Sometime later, she remembered and brought the towels, cheeks flaming because he could not help knowing. Keeping her eyes down, she asked him in halting, embarrassed words to keep her secret, not to tell the mama-*san* she had been a woman who had never known a man before.

That was not the ending, but a beginning. He didn't leave her, but petted her like a child, and they talked far into the star-kissed night, not noticing the slammed doors, the giggles, the drunken laughter of the house around them. They were snug in their own fairytale house, content with each other.

Mama-*san* was pleased, because Brad paid well, because her new girl had a steady customer for day and night. Sueko was ecstatic. This then, was love, this coming together in hungry passion, this soft joy in being close to the man. There was much to learn about each other, and they had held nothing back, told no lies. The world was too full of light and laughter for lies, for any foreboding shadow to cast its darkness over them.

He talked to her of his country, allowed the pent-up violence to leak harmlessly out of him, the coiled and deadly hate that had been ground harshly into his being with the cruel dirt of Korea. He was young, as she was young, and yet aged somehow beyond her by the things he had seen and done. Sueko drew him to her to soothe him, to absorb some of the bitterness so that he would not have so much to carry.

They were happy. They ran skipping down streets like children; they haggled with shopkeepers like newlyweds; they wrestled, they danced, they ate and drank of each other. Happy. The outskirts of Tokyo were dressed in new Spring green, the parks a carnival of insanely blooming cherry trees. Happy.

She didn't ask Brad how long he would be a patient in the hospital; he would tell her if he wished. She didn't question him on the chances of his being shipped home. That, too, was a matter best left to Brad. Sueko was only a woman in love, a woman loved in return, and nothing else mattered.

Hardened, more cynical girls at the New Opal told her she was a fool, that she should make the American sergeant set her up in a small house of her own, that she should ask him for presents and more money. Sueko refused to listen, even when they told her that he would vanish some day and leave her alone.

Yet deep within herself, she knew this was true. But she didn't expect it to happen so soon.

Sueko sensed it in Brad when he came to her that last night. She waited for him to tell her, to say something, anything. He didn't. He talked only of college, and of war, and about things that had little meaning for her. A coldness grew in her belly, knots in her breasts. He was going to leave her.

She didn't let him know that she understood this. She made love to him as before, being pliable, coiling about his huge, hard body in warm desire. Perhaps she was a bit more aggressive, a little more demanding of him. Sueko couldn't be blamed for this. Women say goodbye in the only way they know.

Almost, she had allowed him to see it, in the morning. Her tears wouldn't hold themselves back, no matter how hard she tried. She felt them tremble upon her lashes when she kissed him the last time, but he didn't say anything about them.

The door closed. His boots moved across the silent courtyard, one still a little uncertain. He was gone, and she could not call him back. Only then did Sueko let the tears flow free. She was entitled to that much.

Time became a slow old man, dragging listless feet across the months, the years. There were other customers, for there had to be. Young ones with money clutched in thin hands; old ones smelling of other wives; men who were not men at all, but unhappy and malformed women; men who were jackals paying for helplessness. Some kind, some cruel. All strangers.

Often, Sueko thought of the knife, of the time-honored leap into the cold and jagged crater of *Fujisan* where countless miserable lovers had died. But always, there remained the hunched old woman with the slowing heart who talked to a husband's ashes—a half-crazed boy muttering of vanished glories of the Emperor, a girl protesting that school was a waste of time when she could be earning money the way Sueko did. Three *giri* . . . three duties no Japanese could ignore.

One evening a sergeant brought her a letter. At first, she didn't understand, wouldn't allow herself to hope. But it was from Brad, a letter from Brad. She hurried to a translator, to one of those men in little shops who make a living from reading and writing letters in English, sad and often lying missives that are tenuous threads binding Japanese girls and American soldiers.

There had been no promises enclosed—only stumbling regrets and half-hearted explanations about his family, his duty to them. Brad was sorry. Sueko folded the letter carefully, took it to her room and placed it in the laquered dresser with its spangled mirror. Then she went to bed with the sergeant who had delivered it.

A week later, she was back at the translator's, ignoring his cynical smile. She told him what she wanted to say, and the man wrote it all down. Sueko paid him and mailed the letter, as she was to mail many others. None of them were ever answered. Brad was sorry.

The madam at the New Opal Hotel was not. She was happy that Sueko had come to her senses, that she drank more port wine, urged more soldiers to spend money. Sueko Kamiya was the New Opal's best girl, her dainty loveliness attracting more customers willing to pay higher prices. And these were not "short-time" customers, but men who returned again and again, men drawn to the sad beauty of the girl.

Until the rich and powerful *yami-chan* discovered her; until the black market chief Kai Watanabe developed bigger plans for her. In her room, he talked to Sueko and she listened. She refused to spy on American officers. Kai beat her until she agreed; even then, she would not have accepted—but there were the other Kamiyas, all vulnerable, all easily reached.

Outside the house, a car door slammed. Voices; gruff laughter. Sueko got to her feet, checked her appearance in a mirror. Poised, serene, she waited in the living room. The colonel had friends with him; he would expect her to be gracious, charming. He needed the envy of other men.

Her colonel; her *man*. Sueko's head ached. What else was there? *Who* else was there?

CHAPTER XIII

The shopping center was a mass of moving colors, even in the daytime. Beth parked the car at the edge of it, on a side street off Ize Zaki Cho. Brad climbed out, threw one look at the Sex Drug Store across the way, and passed on. He was to meet Johnny Kojima at the shop that sold pearls still in the oyster.

They found the place a block into the center, on the right. A large aerated tank sat atop a counter, stocked with greyblack pearl oysters shipped up from the Island of Honshu and Mikimoto's farms there.

The sign said: "Pick your own oyster—500 Yen. At least one pearl guaranteed."

Brad touched Beth's hand. "Maybe we ought to make like tourists. I don't see the man I'm supposed to meet. Do you like pearls?"

Beth managed a shaken smile. "They intrigue me. May I shop around?"

She stood up well under strain, Brad thought. The affair in Tokyo, the sudden attack upon her in her own home, and the memory of the dead man still sprawled in her locked bedroom. The servants knew about the battle; they hadn't seen the corpse. A prowler, Beth told them, frightened off. Brad wondered how long that story would hold up.

"This one," Beth said, pointing, "and the one in the corner."

While the shopgirl reached into the briny tank, Brad checked the busy street. If the CIC agent was going to be on time, he had about four minutes. Then what? Brad needed another lead, a clue as to where to look next; he wanted to find out just how hot he was in Tokyo. But he'd already decided not to tell Kojima about the killing. The Army might get mixed up in it, with enough resultant red tape to keep Brad tied down for weeks. He couldn't reach Sueko that way.

And he had to get to her, talk to her and try to explain. He'd beg her to come with him, to some place where they could try together to erase the past, to make the nine intervening years as if they'd never been.

Out of the practically all-Japanese crowd, Johnny Kojima suddenly stood at Brad's elbow. "*Ohio gozaimasta,*" he said, "and a good morning to Dayton and Columbus, too. You look like you got caught in a *Kamikaze* raid."

The agent looked over at Beth, at the shopgirl knifing open pearl oysters, then back at Brad. "But it's a sick typhoon that blows up no good, eh?"

Kojima brought a bulky package out from under one arm, handed it to Brad. "I got these clothes from your room. Thought you might need a change. Ize Zaki Cho doesn't make suits big enough for you."

Brad took the package. "Find anything else in my room?"

Kojima grinned. "You wouldn't want me to waste the taxpayers' money, would you? They paid to send me to lock-picking class, you know. Can't get out of practice." In fluent, rapid Japanese, he said something to the shopgirl. The girl glanced at Brad, answered, and pointed to the rear of the store.

"Slip her a hundred Yen as you go," Kojima said. "She said you could change in back. And—introduce me to the lady?"

Brad hesitated, not wanting to involve Beth any deeper than she already was. "This is Beth," he said, omitting the last name. "Beth, Johnny Kojima. He's on my side."

101

"And happy about it," Kojima said. "You should have seen this guy in action against the Lions. I collected enough bets to keep me in fortune cookies for an entire semester. Or maybe you *did* see him?"

"He has one trouble," Brad said. "He's nosy. Excuse me a minute."

When Brad was gone, Kojima waited until the shopgirl had brought out two pearls and moved down the counter to polish them in cotton. Then he said, "Have you known Brad Saxon very long?"

Beth smiled. "Long enough."

"A man of action," Kojima mused. "You don't have to know him long to find that out." He was looking at Beth and finding her somehow familiar; he filed that fact in the back of his mind for future reference. Whoever she was, wherever he'd met her before, she was one hell of a good-looking woman, and not easy to forget. Brad Saxon was a lucky guy. If his luck held out.

They waited for Brad to come out of the back room. Kojima glanced often over his shoulder while he pretended to be interested in the souvenir counter. Any minute now.

"At least I feel better," Brad said.

"Better than that, pretty soon," Kojima said. "Keep an eye on the drug store. Your buddy Hara is about to knock it off."

Brad frowned. "But—"

"But we lose a place we know about? Not really. The big wheel is smart enough to know *we* know about it."

"Then why raid it?"

Kojima shrugged. "Hara figures to hit a certain big wheel in the pocket again—like you did to the House of All Nations. When the big man is hurt enough, he'll come out swinging."

Brad remembered the Judo man turning cold and stiff in Beth's house. Maybe Kai had already started swinging.

102

A whistle shrilled down the block. Little efficient men moved in on the drug store, a fence of them folding in upon itself with the store as a focal point. A silence fell upon the rest of the street, a tense quiet that was a hangover from the days of the dreaded Imperial Police, when all people walked in fear.

Brad watched clerks being hauled out of the store and tossed into vans. There didn't seem to be any resistance, but an explosion rocked the building. Its windows puffed out; a cloud of smoke snaked from the door. Hara's men were making a mess of the place.

Mr. Hara must be supervising the operation himself, Brad thought, and decided that he didn't want to see the Japanese at the moment. There'd be too many questions to answer. Brad nudged Kojima.

"I'm still trying to find the girl. Any more ideas?"

Kojima nodded. "About twenty miles from here is the 'Little Pentagon,' Camp Zama. A village called Sobudai-mae is just outside it. Try a ginmill named the Club Naha, but watch yourself. After this raid, the big wheel is going to start playing rough."

"Yeah," Brad said, and dropped bills on the counter to pay for the pearls and use of the back room. He hurried Beth out of the shop and down the street to her car.

They were just pulling away from the curb when Brad saw the slight, schoolteacherish form of Hara trotting across the street toward them. "Step on it," he told Beth.

He looked back, made out Hara jotting something into a notebook before the crowd closed him in. Brad settled himself in the seat, feeling the hardness of the .25 automatic in his coat pocket. That was another item he hadn't told the CICI agent about. A pea-shooter, but it might come in handy. A couple of more deaths couldn't get him into any additional trouble. Killing was like pregnancy—no such thing as a little bit of it.

103

Beth was driving carefully, watching for the sudden darting of bicycles, wary of plodding honey-wagons that might wheel illogically into the highway. Brad looked at her profile, the cleanly modeled features, the firm, ripe set of her mouth. He wasn't sure exactly what he felt for Beth. She was a lot of woman, exciting and passionate, full-bodied and beautiful. And she'd proven her courage. Maybe, if he'd met her in the States, known her during the years he'd been seeking someone to fill the emptiness—

But he hadn't, and the nearness of Sueko was a barrier between them. Only Sueko, not Beth's husband; not the angry, defensive gesture she'd made by turning prostitute. Brad thought he might have loved Beth Buckley, if circumstances had been different.

As it was, he was going to have to use her and just say thanks. Beth deserved more than that, more than the rotten breaks she'd gotten from her husband.

They were on the open road now, rice paddies and dry farms flashing by the car windows. Beth asked if he wanted a guided tour. Her voice was emotionless, but Brad sensed the taut emotions underlying her forced lightness.

"Do you know the village Kojima mentioned?"

"Jerry—my husband was stationed at Zama before being transferred to Tokyo. I know it. Most Army wives do. Six shops and about forty bars."

"The Club Naha?"

"We'll find it. Sobudai-mae isn't very big, although its female population keeps busy."

She added suddenly: "Brad—tell me about your girl; about Sueko."

He sat quietly for awhile, sorting words. "She's special; I've loved her a long time. I was too stupid to realize it before. Now I hope it isn't too late."

"You'll—take her back with you?"

"If she'll have me. Maybe she won't. I just walked out on her."

Beth's mouth trembled. "She'll have you, dammit."

"Beth, I—"

"I know. You warned me. Silly of me, isn't it?"

Brad's jaw muscles tightened. "What can I say?"

Beth lifted her chin. "Let's change the subject. What are we going to do about—the man in my bedroom?"

"We won't get back until after dark. Your house isn't far from the bay. I'll carry him down there and drop him in. There shouldn't be anything to connect him to us, to your place."

"Just—just drop him in?"

"He was a hired killer, Beth. Don't waste regrets on him."

Brad didn't explain that regret was for other kinds of men, for kids shot down in a war they didn't even understand, for dedicated young lieutenants beaten to death by communist gun butts, for bone-tired and sleepless commanders trying to hold a thinly-stretched line against a horde of butchers. These were the men to feel sorry for, not savage little animals willing to murder for money.

The village of Sobudai-mae lifted out of farmland —a cluster of shacks around a railroad station, a florist shop on the highway, a taxi stand, bars with beds in their back rooms. Beth swung the car around corners, driving slowly, looking at the signs. They found the place on a gravel-dirt street. The Club Naha was a weary clapboard building, its garish sign a tired invitation to carouse with "Beautiful Girls—No Cover Charge."

They went inside, pausing to let their eyes adjust to semi-darkness. The Naha was a carbon copy of a thousand other bars in Japan, paper-maché palm trees, clothless tables, a scarred drink counter, the inevitable record player with its stacks of scratched platters. At one table, two girls were playing *Goh*. They looked up at Brad, saw the woman with him, and went back to their game, their hair up in curlers, their bodies shapeless in loose kimonos.

105

The place smelled of old perfume and stale beer, of road dust and spilled whisky and cigaret butts. The woman behind the bar was heavy, her face carefully painted on, her oldwise eyes crinkling.

"Scotch okay for you?" Brad asked Beth.

"Anything," she said.

"Two Scotches with water," Brad said, and wondered what this club had to do with Kai Watanabe and Sueko. Maybe she had once worked here, killing time with a *Goh* board like the girls over there, until the nightly influx of GIs came.

They tossed off their drinks, had another round. "You talk to the madam," Beth suggested. "I'll try the girls. Being approached by a 'roundeye' woman always shakes them up, and maybe they'll say something."

"Beth, you don't have to—"

"Don't be an idiot. You can use any help you can get. Besides, those girls and I have something in common, remember?"

"*Nan-deska?*" The house mama-*san* wanted to know what was going on.

"No sweat, mama-*san*," Brad told her, and placed some thousand-Yen notes on the bar. "A tip—if you tell me something."

Her eyes flickered. "You want know about girl?"

"Not just any girl. One named Sueko—Kamiya Sueko."

"No got." She watched the money.

"How about a man—Kai—Watanabe Kai?"

The quick, indrawn breath warned him, the hissing sound Japanese make when they are surprised. "No understand."

"The hell you don't."

Brad slid off the barstool, picked it up. It had thin castiron legs, a cheaply padded cushion. The madam retreated to her row of whisky bottles. Brad held the stool for her to see, tightened his hands upon the legs, swelled his shoulders and bent the iron double. He

106

put the twisted metal on the bar. "You want me to do this to the Club Naha—*all* of it?"

The woman hissed. "No understand."

"Okay," Brad said, and took a grip on the bar itself. The heavy counter would make a satisfying smash into the liquor stock.

A calm voice at his back stopped him, made him drop his hands. "You can destroy the place if you wish, Mr. Saxon. It doesn't belong to the woman, and she won't tell you anything."

Mr. Hara stepped up beside Brad. "You haven't been cooperating."

Brad motioned for more drinks. The woman's hand was shaking as she poured them. "I told you," Brad said, "I'm only interested in finding the girl; nothing else."

"Not even in a dead man in Mrs. Buckley's home?"

Somehow, Hara knew about that, and who Beth was. The question now was, what was he going to do about it?

CHAPTER XIV

At her maid's mute signal, Sueko excused herself from the party. They wouldn't miss her for a few minutes. Not with the extra girls she'd sent for. The colonel included such entertainment for his guests, liked to play the open-handed baron dispensing largess and favors to his friends. The friends would, of course, be called upon sometime to repay him. Not in money, but perhaps in the proper words in the right quarters, in advance information concerning investments where tidy profits might be made.

His friends tonight were civilian traders from America, men who were involved with big import-export corporations. Newly arrived in Japan, they seemed awed by the colonel's broadminded approach to entertainment. One of them wasn't; he had fixed upon Sueko when he was introduced. His eyes hadn't left her for a moment. She felt them upon her as she walked into the kitchen. There would be trouble with that man tonight. She hoped the colonel wouldn't insist that she sleep with him.

Sueko stepped outside, beyond the kitchen door. She pulled in a sharp breath when she saw Saburo's face, bloated out of porportion, blackened.

"Saburo—"

"Money," he said, forming words with difficulty. "For the doctor."

"How—what—"

He limped over to her, his eyes brimming with hate and hurt. "Bring some money."

"But how did it happen? Oh Saburo—I warned you about staying with Kai—"

He spat. "You *warned* me. What right have you got to tell me anything?"

Sueko flinched back from him. "Please—"

"Just do as I say. Your foreign lover won't miss the money; you earn it."

Saburo's spite was a thing she had to bear; she was the elder and he was her responsibility. "You're hurt. Come inside—"

"And cringe in the kitchen like a servant? Maybe you've forgotten you're Japanese; *I* haven't. I wouldn't set foot inside the foreign dog's house."

"But you'll take his money. Why doesn't your good *Japanese* friend help you? You do enough of Kai's filthy work."

He lifted a hand to strike her. Sueko stood still, unafraid.

Saburo dropped his hand, snarled at her. "I work for Japan—for the Party—for anyone who will help drive the Yankee butchers out of our country."

"Kai uses you, that's all," She said. "Just as he uses everyone else. When he's through with you, he'll throw you away."

"Like your great love threw you away? Your *first* great love, I mean—your wonderful Yankee sergeant?"

Sueko took a step back, staring at her brother. "Why—why do you speak of him now?"

"I'll tell you why," Saburo raged at her. "Because *he* did this to me! He tried to kill me! He beat a helpless cripple—he—"

The garden rocked around Sueko, heaved under her feet. Saburo must be lying. Brad—Brad *here?* Back in Japan? He couldn't be. And yet—She fought for control, focused upon Saburo's swollen, insanely twisted face. Long ago, Saburo had hated Brad without ever seeing him, without ever having met him, loathed him because he was the symbol of defeat and shame, his sister's betrayer.

109

Through stiff, numb lips, Sueko cut into her brother's tirade. "Is—is he here? Tell me, Saburo—is Brad in Japan?"

He cursed her. "I told you. He was rutting in the House of All Nations—buying women to hurt them—I tried to—"

"You lie," she said. "Kai brought me there for some reason. Did you know that?"

Saburo looked away. "I—I didn't—"

The mirror exploding, Sueko remembered. The hoarse shouting of her name, while Kai dragged her swiftly out of the house.

An uproar following them. Brad. Brad had been there, close enough for her to touch.

"Wait," Saburo said. "My face, my jaw—I need a doctor."

Sueko brushed his hand away. "You will not die, although I think it might have been better if you had, long ago. *You* are the son of the Kamiya family. I am only a woman."

"The money—"

Coldly, Sueko faced him. "You knew how I felt about Brad. You didn't tell me he had returned. You and Kai had some reason not to tell me. All right, then. Go to Kai for your money. I have none for you."

"Sueko—"

She turned her back upon him and walked away, realizing that she should have done it long before. He might have done something for himself then. Perhaps now it was too late for Saburo, but it was no longer too late for herself. She had lived the lives of others for the past nine years, ever since Brad had gone away. Maybe she could begin to live her own life now. It was a strange feeling to even think of it.

Blindly, she hurried through the kitchen and across the living room. Some of the men were dancing clumsily with Japanese girls, and she threaded through them without a word, without a glance at the colonel. In the bedroom, she brought a bag out

110

of the closet, and was throwing clothes into it as she tried to think. Brad had come back. She didn't know why, and she didn't care. He was back.

She would call every hotel in Tokyo until she found him. In minutes, she could be in the Ginza district. Her hands quivered on the bag lock. Her jewelry, she thought. She wouldn't leave that; she'd have to sell it to live. Brad. Brad.

The door slammed open and shut behind her. Sueko turned. She'd forgotten the party, the colonel.

"What the hell are you up to?" he demanded. "Guest out there—and a special one. Saunders likes you—important man—told him I was broad-minded. Hell, it won't make any difference to you—one man or another."

He saw the open bag on the bed, the jewelry box she held. His slack mouth gaped at her. "What the hell—"

"I'm leaving you," she said in careful English. "Now, tonight."

His face reddened. "*What?* Leaving *me?* You little wench—"

"I will not thank you for the things you have given me," Sueko said. "I was told that I have earned them. I have slept with your friends, and with you." She picked up the bag.

"Oh no," he muttered. "Oh no. No Jap wench is going to walk out on *me*. Not until I get ready to throw you out. You hear, Sueko? Not until I *kick* you out!"

"Please," she said, and started around him.

He back-handed her across the mouth. Sueko fell across the bed, slid off atop the suitcase. She pulled herself up and saw him locking the door. When he turned back to her, she realized he was drunker than usual, and fumbling at his belt.

"No," she said, and left the suitcase on the floor as she darted for the window with her jewelry box clutched to her.

111

The belt buckle lanced with exquisite agony into her back. He was upon her, hurling her back into the room. "Damn you—damn you. You dirty little—"

He was drunk and mean, and he'd been hurt in a tender spot, his ego. He was the all-powerful white man, scorned by a woman of an inferior race—an officer whose word was law to thousands of men; a bloated, swollen ego that wouldn't accept anything that didn't go its way.

"You stay," he shouted at her as she lay on the floor at his feet, the sight of her trim golden thighs only inflaming him more. "You stay! and you do as I tell you. Now get up and change your dress. You'll bed my friend Saunders tonight and you'll like it—do you hear? And you'll crawl to me and beg me to forgive you. Or—or I'll see that you're locked in jail until you're an old, old woman."

Painfully, Sueko crawled off the floor. Her dress was wet in back where the belt buckle had chewed into her flesh. He had used the belt on her before this, but never the buckle. Jail, he said. Perhaps he could put her there. He was a man with many friends; all of them owed him something—Japanese and Americans alike. Perhaps the colonel could see that she went to prison on some false charge. And maybe he couldn't.

She picked her words. "You talk of jail. All right. You like to talk, colonel. Too much. You say things the CIC wouldn't like you to say."

His face paled; his fist clenched the belt. "You can't prove that."

"Others will prove it," she said, and went to a certain place in the bedroom wall. "Look."

Sueko pressed a section of wallboard, swung it out on silent, oiled hinges to expose the miniature tape recorder. "This is only one machine. There are others. Ever since I have been in this house, the machines have listened."

He choked. "You—you—"

112

Sueko continued. "Many reels have already been delivered to—to a man who uses them. Now, colonel; if you talk of jail, you mean for both of us."

The colonel swallowed; his heavy brows pulled down in knots. She saw that he was thinking furiously, trying to clear the cobwebs of whisky out of his mind. Sueko knew enough about the Army to understand how frightened he was, what exposure of his careless words over the months would mean to the CIC. A court-martial would break him, send him to prison for a long time.

"Now, Sueko," he said. "Wait a minute—if it's money you want—"

"No money. Just let me leave."

He grabbed her. "And blackmail me for the rest of my life? The hell I will! I know how to handle you—how to get rid of you!"

She fought his hands away from her throat. "The reels—"

He slammed a fist into her stomach. She gasped for air, hearing him through a haze of pain. "You were working for somebody," he said. "You didn't try to get money from me, so it's something else. I'll find out who you took those tapes to—I'll find out."

His hands were busy at her ankles, jerking the belt tight about them. Sueko tried to sit up as he tore a pillowcase from the bed, ripped it into strips. He punched her again, and she lay quietly, because she was too small to fight him.

Froth flecked the corners of his mouth as he tied her hands. "You'll get taken care of, my dear. Not here; not where you can ever be traced to this house. Now—there—just wait awhile, and pray to your ugly Shinto demons. I have guests, remember? They'll be sorry you were taken so ill—especially Saunders. But he'll understand. I'll tell him you'll be available later."

Giggling drunkenly, he unlocked the door and went out. Sueko heard the metallic click of the key as he turned it in the lock again. She began to struggle, to try and squirm out of the strips of pillow case that tied her arms to the bed. Straining, arching her back and throwing all of her small strength into the effort, she fought to free herself.

Over and over, Sueko tensed herself, yanked at her bonds, tried desperately to kick. It was no good. Gasping, she lay upon the bed, unconscious of the passage of time, knowing only that she had to get out of the house and find Brad.

It may have been an hour, perhaps less, before the door opened. Eyes stretched wide, Sueko stared at the man crossing the room and opening the window. In mangled Japanese, he said something to someone waiting outside. From the living room, the sounds of the party grew in volume.

The man stood over her, his hairy hands laced across his puffed belly. "Well, well," Captain Getty said. "I told you I'd be around when the colonel was ready to boot you out. You're gonna' be sorry you got snotty with me, Sueko—damned sorry."

CHAPTER XV

The body of the man Brad had killed was gone, sheeted and carried away by members of Mr. Hara's Secret Police. The bedroom door was closed, and they sat like casual friends around the coffee table in the living room—Hara, Beth and Brad. They were anything but casual. Only the Japanese seemed imperturbable.

"Dammit," Brad said, "I told you how it was. I killed the man in self-defense. He attacked Mrs. Buckley; he jumped me."

Hara nodded. "Yes. He was a wanted man, a dangerous one. You have done Japan a service, Mr. Saxon."

"Then what the hell are we still sitting around for? You hauled me out of the Club Naha. If I can't find out about Sueko there, you could let me go back to the House of All Nations."

"That Naha is now padlocked," Hara said. "Violations of fire precautions. It will make no more money for our mutual enemy."

"Hara," Brad said, "you're beginning to irritate me. Damned near everybody in Japan is beginning to irritate me. Pretty soon I'm going to blow up in somebody's face."

Hara allowed himself a smile. "Miss Kamiya must be flattered by such stubborn devotion. But, please—allow me to state my case before you—ahh—blow up."

"If you hurry," Brad said.

115

Hara expanded his smile to include Beth. "A fine home, Mrs. Buckley. I fail to understand why—"

She made it easier for him. "Why I worked at the House of All Nations? I'll tell you Mr. Hara."

Beth did, omitting nothing, sparing herself nothing in the telling.

Brad shifted uncomfortably as she sketched in details of her unhappy life with her husband, her illogical attempts to strike back at him by selling her body to any man who had the price, how, once in, she couldn't get out. Her voice was even, but Brad saw the whiteness of her clenched fingers.

"Then you are alienated from your husband, the colonel? You know little of his daily life, his habits?"

Beth chewed her lip. "If you mean knowing about his Japanese mistress, I do. Otherwise, we're strangers. Jerry hasn't been home for a week."

"Ah yes," Hara mused. "The house in Tokyo. It had to be something like that. An unexpected source—"

"Get with it, Hara," Brad said. "I'm in a hurry."

"Very well. Mr. Saxon, perhaps you're aware of the unrest in this country? The violent riots last year which caused the government to lose much face? I see you remember those; your president—well; to the point: we have many greedy and bitter people, as all nations have. Some work for the Russians in the mistaken belief that all will be changed, that all will have money and power and two rice bowls. Some, like Kai Watanabe, are not so easily fooled. They operate with one eye on the possible future, one on present financial gains. These are the dangerous men, those who sell your nation's secrets and mine."

Brad listened to Hara explain that he, and most of the level heads in Japan, felt the country's future to be tied with the United States. To that end, the Secret Police worked to block the shipment of information and U. S. "green money." The job was made difficult by the present Status of Forces Agreement. Of course, Japan was not officially occupied any more, still—

"You can't step on too many American toes, is that it?" Brad asked.

"Precisely. So we were happy to see you appear, searching for a girl we know is connected with Watanabe—since you could, as you put it—step on toes without causing an incident.

Watanabe has some influential friends in the military. And may I say you gave us the idea of wrecking his businesses? Our minds seldom work so directly."

"And," Brad said, "You've been talking to Johnny Kojima."

"The Nisei officer. A most cooperative man. His position is the reverse of mine. He cannot involve himself with Japanese Nationals, while I—"

"Okay," Brad said, "okay. You said that Sueko was mixed up with Watanabe; I'll admit that. I saw her with him. But that doesn't mean she's a part of this spy system. How do you know that?"

Hara smiled sadly. "I did not, until I saw you with Mrs. Buckley this morning. I checked out the license number of her car, put others to investigating her husband. Now I know Miss Kamiya passes information to Watanabe. Everything dropped into place like one of our wooden puzzles. Find the key section, and the rest is simple."

"Dammit—"

Hara lifted one hand. "Miss Kamiya was the connecting section of the puzzle. In turn, she leads us to Colonel Jeremy Buckley."

Beth's husband? Brad heaved himself out of his chair. What did this Buckley guy have to do with it? He looked at Beth's white face, saw nothing, and threw the question at Hara.

"Why," Hara explained, "Miss Kamiya lives in the Tokyo house as Colonel's Buckley's mistress. Your pardon, Mrs. Buckley."

Beth clenched the arms of her chair. "Jerry's mis-

117

tress—Sueko—oh, believe me, Brad, I didn't know. I had no idea that the girl you're looking for—"

"I believe you," Brad said. "Okay. So she's his shackmate. Now tell me where he keeps her."

Hara lifted his hands apologetically to Beth.

"If you will confirm my suspicions, search the house, perhaps question the colonel a bit. I would have to get a warrant, bring in the American CIC, the MPs. My bird will have flown by then. And—Mr. Saxon—Miss Kamiya must also tell you all she knows."

Brad thought it over. A bigmouthed colonel, spilling military information that dribbled across the Yellow Sea to China, that channeled through Peiping to Moscow. Sure, he'd make him talk, tear the damned house down, if that was what Hara wanted. But there was Beth to be considered. The man was her husband.

"Beth?"

"It's all right with me," she said. "Sometime just before dawn this morning, lying there close to you, I cut Jerry Buckley out of my life. It's all right with me if you draw and quarter him."

Hara coughed delicately. "Nothing so drastic, Mrs. Buckley. The colonel and Miss Kamiya are both in Tokyo at the moment, Mr. Saxon. Shall we—"

"Just a minute," Brad said. "What kind of deal do you intend giving Sueko? If she's handling military information, she's been pushed into it. Kai has some kind of hold on her. I didn't come across half the world to see her get tried for treason."

Hara built an arch of his thin, parchment fingers, peered at Brad over it. "You believe this—that the girl betrays our countries because she must, and not for money?"

Brad took a deep breath. Nine years could make a lot of changes in anybody, much less in a girl who had to struggle for a living any way she knew how. But if he didn't believe in her now, in the basic honesty of her, he'd might as well quit and go home.

"Yes," he said, "I think Kai is threatening her—and her family."

Mr. Hara stood up. "Very well. Here is my deal, then: if such is the case, you may take Miss Kamiya away. If it is *not* the case—" he left the rest unsaid, but Brad understood. Swiftly and effortlessly, Sueko would disappear.

Nobody would ever see her again, Case closed.

"Let's go," Brad said. "I guess you've got a car outside."

"*My* car," Beth cut in. "I'm with you, remember? And Jerry might say things to me even you couldn't beat out of him.

CHAPTER XVI

Getty watched nondescript Japanese fishermen unloading the long, heavily-wrapped bundle from the truck. Faint, damp wisps of fog clung to the dock, spread listlessly out across the calm waters of Tokyo Bay. The fog was not as thick as he'd like it to be, but is would serve as pretty fair camouflage. Not that he expected trouble; he was just a careful man. He hadn't gotten this far in the Service by being reckless.

He was off-duty, but the comforting weight of the snub .38 Special in his hip pocket reminded him that he was protected as usual, and prepared for any emergency. Plus the six men who'd worked at odd jobs for him from time to time. His own police force. Getty wet thick lips in smug satisfaction. Let other men buck for high-ranking troop commands, or study and sweat for administration posts. Getty had long ago learned that the most lucrative job in the Army was his own.

Oh, maybe a Provost Marshal knocked down a little more graft, in certain areas. But the Provost was chained down more, too; surrounded by desk work and responsibilities. Getty smirked into the fog; hell —some of them were even honest. They'd creak out of the Army on their lousy retirement pay and live on hamburger and beans the rest of their lives.

Not Ward Getty. There was a tidy bank deposit box in California; its contents grew every month— payoffs from prostitutes, slim sheafs of bills from madams who didn't want their bars thrown Off

Limits; shakedown money from black market boys, from GIs peddling NCO Club whisky—money channeling itself to him from half a hundred sources. When Getty shed the uniform, he'd coast along on sirloin and champagne.

And there were other advantages. Free women and booze; fancy meals hotels begged him to eat; suits tailored in Hong Kong—"presents" from Air Force pilots who knew he had them in a bind for running in illicit gold.

Favors from colonels and generals, too; guys who wanted this regulation winked at, that regulation bypassed. Like Colonel Buckley. Once this little job for the colonel was finished, he'd have the hook so deep in Buckley that the colonel would never wriggle free of it. The colonel didn't know it yet, but he'd pay off the rest of his life. A nice bonus to be added to the retirement fund, coming in with clockwork regularity.

Getty patted his belly, stood on the dock and looked both ways along its deserted stillness. Fine; no late fisherman nosing around. The Omori district wharves were generally empty at this time of night, and the tide beginning its slow rise. Getty glanced to his left, saw the dark bulk of the Omori Transformer Station; to his right for the Nihou Steel Company landmark. Industrial area; small fishing junks, crab boats. He'd chosen his anchorage well. Out there in the dark, far enough away so that no one could hear even the most frenzied screams, the *Tatsu Temma* swung at its rusty chain.

He had used the junk before—for the special kind of parties he liked to stage when there was time and opportunity; as a safe drop for tinned kilos of heroin to be wholesaled to the street runners. It was the perfect setup for what he had in mind now.

A man hissed at him from the skiff. Getty grunted in return and waddled to the end of the dock. Cautiously, he climbed down into the unsteady small boat. Only when he was firmly seated did he signal

121

the pair at the sweep to shove off. The canvas-wrapped bundle lay with one end close to his feet. Getty leaned forward and patted it. The bundle writhed. Getty smiled into the night and settled back. The high-nosed wench would do more than squirm before he was through with her. Sueko had a few surprises coming—interestingly painful surprises.

Minutes later, the boat thumped into the side of the *Tatsu Temma,* jolting the "Dragon Junk" with a slap that made her timbers creak. Getty cursed. Japs were supposed to be great seamen, but they never failed to ram each other, day or night, small boats or big ships. Getty waited until the boat was tied, then inched up to the low gunwale of the junk and climbed over. Below decks the *Tatsu* was no ordinary fishing junk, but a party boat, with a hold far larger than it appeared from above.

At a carven teakwood bar, Getty treated himself to a glass of excellent cognac and selected a rich cigar from a cunningly built-in dispenser. He padded over to a thickly heaped pile of brocade pillows and lowered himself upon them. Here, Ward Getty was king; an emperor on his couch at the end of a private arena where his slaves performed for him, jumped and cringed at the snap of his fingers. His men struggled down the ladder with Sueko.

"Cut her free," he ordered, "remove the gag and strap her to the rings."

As they worked at the canvas, Getty looked at the ringbolts set solidly into the timbers—two high, two low. The girl would be erect there, spread-eagled and helpless, her wrists and ankles lashed. Very soon, she'd see what it meant to spit at Ward Getty—to threaten him. Anticipation rose within him, making his mouth dry, sending tremors through his tightening belly. He reminded himself that he mustn't hurry, that there was plenty of time to enjoy each quiver of her body. Getty had another cognac, licked sensuously at his cigar. Plenty of time.

122

When they lifted her to the ringbolts, Sueko's small face was smudged and streaked with tears and dirt, the glistening masses of her hair tumbled, disheveled. Her dress was stained, wrinkled; she had no shoes, and her nylons were torn spiderwebs. In back, blood spotted the dress where the colonel's belt buckle had ripped in. Sueko's mouth was swollen, her eyes puffed. She was still beautiful.

"Okay," Getty said to the men as they stood back from the strung-up girl. "Okay—now get up on deck. Drink *sake* if you want, but some of you keep your eyes open. *Wakaru* . . . understand?"

They understood; they had bound girls like this for the fat captain before, and listened to their screams rocket out through the hatchway and die echoing and unheard on land. He paid well; that was their only concern. They shuffled up the ladder in their straw sandals, thirsty for the barrel of good *sake* kept forward.

Getty climbed off the pillows and went to Sueko, tilting her chin up with a thick forefinger. "You're dirty," he said. "I don't like dirty women. But there's plenty of time. I'll clean you up—first."

Throat clotting, licking at his lips, Getty brought a large pan from the galley, filled it with clear water and found soap and a wash cloth. He placed the things on the deck between her spread ankles. Slowly, then, enjoying the sound of tearing cloth, he ripped her dress away from Sueko's trembling body.

Soft and golden, rays from the overhead lamps played across her flesh, highlighting curves, making delectable shadows of shapely valleys. Almost gently, Getty worked his fingers into the twin cups of Sueko's bra, snapped the catch and let it fall. Her panties were sheer, lace-edged, and held against his hand until he snarled and jerked savagely at them.

"No," he mumbled. "Not too fast, remember? Not too quick; make it last. No need to hurry."

Mercilessly, she was exposed to his eyes, hanging

123

nude and stretched for him. Getty trembled, crooned far back in his throat and stepped back to work out of his own clothing. Sueko closed her eyes. He chuckled wetly at her, and stooped for the wash cloth and soap. Ever so slowly, Getty moved the slickly lathered cloth over her body, cleansing her satiny skin, making a glittering pyramid of sparkling bubbles over each of her taut breasts, trailing his hand across her flinching belly, massaging her hips, washing the strained and gleaming thighs.

From throat to tiny feet, he soaped her, moving around to lather the curve of her back, the dainty, modeled flare of her haunches. Getty thrilled at the feel of her, warmwet and sliding under his hands. He left her diamonded by bubbles while we went to change water in the pan.

Sueko jerked against her bonds as he came back to pour cold water over her. It ran splashing over her breasts, cascaded across her stomach and along her thighs, the curves of her calves, to puddle the wooden deck. She gasped for breath as Getty stood before her, big, shaggy head cocked to one side like some obscenely hungry bird, pouched eyes bright in anticipation.

"Now," he said. "You're bathed and clean for me. Don't you want to thank me, Sueko?"

She spat at him. Getty lifted one hairy hand and wiped his cheek. "You're ungrateful. Well—that will change; that will change. You have a lovely body, Sueko. All polished and shining. You look almost virginal, like a child prematurely developed. Ahh—but the firm arch of your breasts, the ripeness of your thighs. These aren't childlike."

"Pig!" she said through clenched teeth, and added other words she had learned from drunken soldiers, lashing him with the words, hurling them into his sweating face with hate and fear.

Getty laughed. His curved fingers wandered scratching through the matted fur on his swollen

124

belly. "It'll be a real pleasure to make you beg, to break your spirit until you whimper and cry."

"Never!" she said, and writhed frantically against the ropes that held her.

Getty moved chuckling to a dragon-painted cabinet, opened it and took out a slim leather whip.

Its haft was thin and switchlike in his damp palm, its lash stretched plaited and snaky. He flicked it, making its tip snap viciously in the air. "Never?" he repeated. "Never?"

He was an expert in the use of that whip, gauging the exact distance it needed to merely kiss the flesh without breaking it needlessly, making it bite with a miniature agony each time it landed. After he tired of picking targets that way, he would put more weight into each stroke, cutting deeper, wetting the lash with blood. But that would come later, much later. Now he snapped his wrist, saw the leather tip serpentine out and brush the darkrose tip of one breast.

Sueko jerked and twisted. "Wait!"

Getty drew the whip back to him, fingered its haft. "So soon? I thought you were stronger, Sueko. Don't give up so quickly. We have all night here together."

"Colonel Buckley—"

"He's finished with you. Remember, I told you he would be. Now you know why I was waiting so patiently."

The whip lanced out, flicked Sueko's other breast. She gasped in pain. "No—I do not mean—do you know *why* he's finished with me?"

Getty shook his head. "It doesn't matter. You're mine, now."

"But it does matter!" Desperately, Sueko tried to find the right words. "His house has recording machines in it—many of them. I—I showed him one, told him what they were used for—how I delivered the little reels with his talk on them."

Getty scratched his stomach with one hand, moved

125

the whip restlessly in the other. So *that* was the reason Buckley had called him in. The colonel's house was tapped, and Sueko had been passing bits of information along to someone else. Hell; he should have known Buckley wouldn't give up the girl unless he was scared spitless by something she'd done or said. Tape recorders planted all over the Tokyo house; well.

"Where did you take the reels, Sueko? Who'd you give 'em to?"

"The—the House of All Nations," she said rapidly. "To Kai Watanabe. They are kept in the kitchen storeroom, behind bags of rice."

Getty frowned. That damned Watanabe. Things began to make sense—Kai steering him onto the Stateside civilian, Brad Saxon, wanting him to scare the big ape out of Japan. Sure, because the guy might have spoiled Kai's setup at the Buckley house by taking away the girl. The sly Nipper had used him to bait Buckley with, in the first place, too. What the hell did Buckley talk about that was so important, that could be converted into cash?

Getty remembered that the colonel's job didn't seem much on the surface, but now that he looked at it carefully, he could see how Buckley might know a lot of things. And Kai had used Ward Getty to get a hand-picked girl next to the colonel.

Thinking hard, Getty suddenly recalled the strange scene in the police station after the Saxon guy had torn up the New Opal Hotel and damned near killed two or three of the madam's bouncers. For no reason that Getty could understand, Saxon had been released —and his scrawny little interpreter with him. What kind of sense did that make? Was Watanabe trying to play both ends against the middle? After all, the tough Nipper hadn't told him a damned thing about Saxon having State Department connections, either.

If he had leaned on Saxon too hard, pressured him through the dried-up DAC girl in the Ambassador's office, the whole thing could have easily blown up in his face. Getty sure as hell didn't want any State Department investigations going on right now—or any other kind, for that matter. If he remained as careful as he had been for these past two years, not calling attention to his operations, not getting too greedy, he could leave the Army a rich and respected man. If not—Leavenworth was a hell of a place to spend twenty or thirty years.

Getty thought about Kai Watanabe and the colonel. Sure he'd done a few jobs for Kai in the past, and Watanabe had steered a few good things his way—that hijacked shipment of happy dust from Red China; those very young and tender girls just fresh off the farms. But Kai always got a piece of the action for himself—maybe more than just a nibble; maybe a whole damned gulp.

It was about time to get Watanabe out of the picture, move in on the guy's operations. The taped reels would be a good start. Once they were missing, the guys who were buying them would be certain to make contact with the MP captain who'd been in on a recent raid. Yeah; and he could make Buckley sweat dollar bills at the same time.

He looked back at the girl. Sueko had been a prize in more than one way. Watching the light shift over her naked body with each gentle roll of the boat, Getty decided that Watanabe and the colonel could wait awhile. He had a lot of tricks to use on Sueko first. She hadn't bought a damned thing with her information—only a few untortured moments.

CHAPTER XVII

A phone call ahead had gathered a knot of Hara's men two blocks away from the house. Beth pulled the car over to them when Hara tapped her shoulder from the back seat. The bespectacled Japanese paused at Brad's window.

"I can keep the local police from answering any calls," he said. "The Military Police are different. You'll remember that? And our agreement?"

Brad nodded. "Just so you don't forget your end. The girl won't be touched, if she's been forced into this business."

Mr. Hara touched his hat. "If she has been forced. Mrs. Buckley?" And he was gone into the waiting group of quietly dressed men on the sidewalk.

"I've seen the house," Beth said, guiding the car into a driveway, "but never the inside. How—what are you going to do, Brad?"

He stared at the lighted windows, heard music and laughter wash out onto the lawn. "I only know one way to move, Beth—that's just to barrel straight ahead. Your husband has Sueko in there. I've got to bring her out, no matter how he feels about it. And I promised Hara I'd do what I could to find who Buckley is working with. I might have to hurt him to do that. If you'd rather wait here for me—"

"I'm coming in," she said. "I don't care what you do to Jerry. He's got it coming. And maybe you haven't noticed yet—but there are a couple of GIs

128

over there watching this car. They won't try to stop us, when I tell them who I am."

Brad opened the car door. "What are GIs doing here?"

Beth looked over at them. "Jerry has a driver assigned to him, and he's usually entertaining visiting firemen. Here they come."

Brad was silent as the sergeants neared, but Beth greeted them. "Good evening; I'm Mrs. Buckley. The colonel is in, I see."

The men glanced at each other. "Ahh—yes mam', but—"

"Thank you," Beth said and took Brad's arm.

A Japanese butler stuttered in the doorway as Beth swept regally past him with Brad at her heels. She hesitated in the foyer, then turned toward the big room off it, where the sounds of revelry were loud. Brad noticed five hats on the hall table—four civilian and one military. The colonel had guests, all right. Mr. Hara hadn't figured on that. Now the guests would just have to take their chances with Buckley. Brad sure as hell wasn't going to let them run out and call the MPs. That reminded him of something, and the telephone wasn't difficult to find. It squatted beside the hats. One swift yank ripped its wires out of the wall. Brad followed Beth into the living room.

If the setting had been different, the scene before them could have been a Roman orgy. A hi-fi thumped and bassoed, swirling its unheard rhythms around a tableau of men and women together on couches and the floor. A nude girl saw them first, and squealed. Men jerked startled faces around; another girl scrabbled for discarded underwear. A highball glass toppled, spilling liquid and ice cubes across the rug.

Beth's face was frozen, without emotion. Brad caught her elbow. "Which one is the colonel?"

She pointed. "The chubby one in the striped shorts; the drunkest one."

"Close the door," Brad said. "Don't open it again."

129

He took the .25 automatic out of his jacket and put it into her hand. Beth nodded.

Brad plowed across the room and kicked the record player off its stand. The sudden silence was almost deafening in itself. "Buckley," Brad said.

The colonel clawed for a robe. "Who—what do you—"

"Be dignified," Beth said from the door. "Officer and gentleman, remember."

Buckley swung glazed eyes. "B-Beth! You—what—"

A big hand closed bitingly into a plump shoulder, snatched the colonel to his feet. "Sueko. Where is Sueko?"

"S-Sueko? I—I don't know what you're—what the hell are you doing in here?" My wife—get out. Both of you, get out before I—"

Brad slapped him, the sound shocking and meaty in the room. Buckley gasped. "Colonel," Brad said softly, "I'm not a patient guy. Once more, where is Sueko?"

A man lunged from the couch, sputtering. "Look here—you can't come in here and—"

Shoving Buckley back, Brad spun and hooked the man on the cheekbone with a fist like a granite block. He bounced once on the couch cushions and slid limply off to the floor. Brad moved in on the staggering colonel, hands cocked, stern-ugly face set stubbornly.

"He—he's crazy!" Buckley screamed. "Insane—he's trying to kill me! Help me—Hioshi! Sergeant!"

"Brad!" Beth's voice halted him. He balanced on the balls of his feet, waiting, watching the colonel's face.

"There's a closet over there," Beth said. "No windows. I think the rest of them will fit in it."

"They'll fit," Brad said, and roared it without turning around: "You heard her!"

They scampered like frightened mice, half-dragging the man who had tried to come at Brad. Beth

130

motioned them into the closet with the steady muzzle of the gun. The girls were sobbing; the men shaking. She slammed the door after them and turned a key.

"Ask him again," she said to Brad.

"Hioshi!" Buckley shrieked. "Sergeant Mills!"

Brad dug a short chop into the man's soft belly, watched him gag and grab at himself. "A sample," Brad said. "The next one might break a couple of ribs. Where is Sueko?"

Buckley's face was green. "D-damn you—I don't know—wait! Don't hit me again!"

Brad didn't want to look at Beth. This cringing white worm was what she was married to—a slob partying and running off at the mouth while other men waited in fox holes for the talk to bounce back at them in bullets.

Beth yelled something garbled as the door crashed inward and threw her into the wall. Spinning around, Brad's feet pumped hard, drove him headlong across the living room to meet the men plunging in. His shoulder caught one, lifted him kicking into the air; a hooked arm cut the other's legs out from under him, whiplashed him into the floor. Rolling, Brad saw the twisted face of the Japanese butler, smashed it with a looping right.

The sergeant driver kicked on the floor, wheezing for breath.

"Don't make me hit you again," Brad said, and left him there.

He caught Buckley trying to get out of the window, slammed him across the kidney and stood over him as he fell back. "I'm through playing, mister. Tell me about Sueko or I start kicking your guts out."

Buckley whimpered. "I—I don't think she—she threatened me, planted tape recorders in this house. I—I might have said some things that could get me into trouble. Please—I don't know who you are—"

Brad lifted one foot, ground it into Buckley's stomach. Eyes bulging, the colonel tugged at it with

131

both hands. "B-Beth! Beth, help me. This man is killing me!"

"Good," she said from across the room. "Remember Mr. Hara, Brad."

"So you talked a lot," Brad said, "maybe bragged about how you handled troop movements, who said this and who said that. And the Reds have got it all. Is that it? The tape recorders, you slob—where are they?"

"One—one's in the bedroom. She—she said there are others. I meant to find them later."

"So much for Hara," Brad said. "Sueko threatened you. Why?"

"Because I wouldn't let her leave. My stomach—"

"And what did you do to her?"

Buckley's mouth tightened; he shook his head. Brad pressed down, leaning more weight into the man's belly.

Buckley gagged, beat his heels against the floor. Brad eased off. "All right," Buckley choked, "all right. She's just a cheap Jap prostitute; I called to somebody, had her taken away."

With one terrifying motion, Brad scooped him up and fastened his hands around the colonel's throat. "Where—damn you—*where?*"

"Y-you're strangling me! Getty has her. I—I didn't tell him to kill her, just—just take her away where she couldn't talk about me."

"Getty? The MP?" Brad shook Buckley like a doll.

"He has a boat in the harbor—off Omori. The—the Dragon Junk, *Tatsu Temma.*"

Stiff-armed, Brad held the cringing man at arm's length. "You slob. An officer; a colonel—a leader. It's a good thing we've got a thousand real officers for every louse like you and Getty, a thousand platoon leaders and company commanders who wouldn't let you wipe their boots. You make me want to throw up—colonel."

Buckley saw it in his face, the hard mouth thinning

132

around its scar, the crooked nose and pitiless eyes. "No! Don't kill me!"

"That's too easy," Brad hissed, "too damned easy for you," and pulled the punch just enough so that Buckley's neck didn't snap from it.

Beth came from the door, stared dry-eyed down at her husband's unconscious body. "You should have killed him."

"No. He'll have a lot of misery facing him—court-martial, disgrace. That will hurt him more. Beth—Omori—you know where that is?"

"I think so. Down Avenue 'A'—do you think he sent Sueko to be murdered?"

Brad pulled her after him. "Hurry—"

Down the hall and out, with Beth stumbling on the steps. Across the yard and into the car; the motor whirring, kicking over. Around the drive where Beth hit the brakes hard. "Damn—of all the times—"

Costumed men leaping and yelling ahead of them, blocking the street, drums hammering, festooned poles swaying.

"What is it?" Brad yelled over the noise. "Plow through them—"

"I can't. One of their wild Shinto celebrations—they're all drunk, fanatical—they'll dance on past in a minute."

Brad leaned over and hit the horn. Its blast was lost in the milling, yelling throng. White capes spinning, flushed faces around the car, teeth gleaming, eyes bright—

He saw the gun muzzle barely in time to chop down on the handle and elbow the car door into it. The blast swung the door back into his shoulder. Brad heeled Beth over onto the seat, kicked himself out of the car and hit the ground on hands and knees. The gun bore gaped down at him. He whipped up and in, hands desperate.

And had the pistol as the killer flew back into the crowd. Something tugged at Brad's sleeve, slapped

133

into the car beside him. In reflex, he fired at a flash, heard a man's high-pitched scream blend with the explosion. The costumed men scattered, dropping banners, forgotten drums skipping behind them. All but four. These crouched over another man on his back, hands lifting to point at Brad. He hit the ground, rolled as the bullets chewed earth up around him, came up to fire once at them before he dove behind the car.

Everything was brightly familiar—time hanging in slow motion, the taste of cordite blown back into his face, the spiteful slap-slap of bullets searching for him, men flitting forward—little men with dark faces and slanting eyes.

One of them scurried around the car, stumbled as Brad's slug caught him in the middle, and hurtled on into a trimmed hedge. He turned though, and plowed a shot into the car. Brad shot him again, once more when he staggered, and damned a small caliber gun.

A flurry of legs and skirt, and Beth sprawled beside him behind the ornamental rockpile that graced the lawn. A slug tore into the shaped cherry tree and whined away in a flurry of green splinters. Beth propped the little pistol with both hands and triggered a shot in return.

"The car!" she screamed. "Brad—they're taking the car!"

He lunged up, snapped a bullet at a moving white robe, and shoved the pistol ahead of him as he dove into the car. The gun clicked. A redwhite flash burst in Brad's face. Blindly, he chopped out with the empty gun, felt it grate into something that fell away. The car was rolling down an incline; he punched a fist against its brake pedal, kicked up to a sitting position on the seat.

"Beth! come on—"

Her .25 popped twice; a heavier gun answered. "I can't!" she yelled. "Go ahead—Sueko may be dying!

Get to her, Brad—straight ahead, turn right to the docks when the street ends. Go ahead, Brad!"

His head spun. Sueko—out in the Bay with Getty; maybe he was lifting her body into the water right now—Sueko—Sueko—

Beth's gun popped; a man yelped.

Beth—Sueko—

The car rolled forward, motor idling. Brad turned to look back at Beth; his foot hit the gas pedal. The car leaped ahead, bounced over a man's body, rocked crazily across the sidewalk. He snatched the wheel, wrestled with it and caught a glimpse of a wave of men running—men with guns in their hands. Beth.

Head low, Brad pointed the car at the line of gunmen, floorboarded it as they scattered out of his path. He was through them, tires squealing, thundering straight ahead on Avenue "A"—flashing toward the Omori docks and a junk somewhere in the bay. Maybe he'd have left Beth behind, anyway, maybe the gut-wrenching tug of Sueko's danger overbalanced anything he felt for Beth Buckley. He didn't know—he just didn't know.

But as he roared the heavy car on into the night, he was certain of one thing. With that sudden line of gunmen bearing down, neither of them would have had a chance. Whether he'd wanted to run out on Beth or not didn't matter now.

CHAPTER XVIII

Colonel Buckley came awake in time to stop the groggy butler from calling police. If the phone had been connected, they'd have already arrived. But the man had been driven back inside the house. Some sort of violence at a street celebration. Buckley held his head.

Frightened and angry, his guests were gone now, but the colonel was too worried to regret losing the business deals that meant. That savage brute standing over him, grinding agonizing weight into his stomach—choking him—beating him. Buckley ached; he was nearly sober; he didn't like it.

His wife standing with a pistol in her hand while the man almost killed him. Beth, looking like an icy and cruel stranger. What had she been doing with that ugly primitive? Why? He made it to the bar, found a bottle and drank deeply without looking at the label. Coughing, he wiped at his mouth and winced.

Buckley couldn't think clearly; so many things crowding in at once. The beating, shaming him in front of important guests; Beth's metamorphosis; Sueko's attempt to leave him, threatening him with blackmail and disgrace. Sueko—gorgeous little wench, trapping him with tape recorders. Buckley drank again, felt the liquor's warmth spreading, pushing back the cold fear.

He had to do something about those recorders— find them, destroy them before somebody else did.

What if somebody talked to the MPs about the brawl here? Buckley's dazed mind sorted through names, came up with a Provost Marshal. The major might help; and he might not. No—better not ask. Who else, then?

Another drink calmed the trembling of his hands, eased the throbbing sore spots in his ribs and jaw. Easy, Buckley told himself, take it easy. He had a lot of friends, many connections. Once those recorders were smashed, a court-martial board would have a hell of a time proving anything.

Blearily, the colonel eyed the bottle he held. Money at home, in the bank; taxes carefully paid on "investment returns." But—and he sat up—the money was in a joint bank account. Beth could draw it out. Well, he'd fix that in the morning. A call to the States, a convincing explanation. But first—first those damned tape recorders.

He wobbled into the bedroom, pawed at the wall, brought out the machine Sueko had shown him. Wheezing, he ripped at its reels, tore them loose and dropped them into a pillowcase. Where else? Back to the living room, of course—other bedrooms, his study where business deals were made. He had to find them all.

Thus protected, then he'd see who was going to push him around. That leering, broken-nose brute had the stamp of an enlisted man on him; he wouldn't be too difficult to find. If regular MP channels couldn't accomplish it, there were other ways. And Beth—placid, easy-going, unexciting Beth. She had to be punished, too; bringing that swine in here, pointing guns. She must have gone mad. That was it—she was crazy. A psychiatrist he knew would testify to that, put her into a locked ward.

The explanation would be simple. She'd broken under the strain of the impending divorce. You understand, gentlemen—we haven't been man and wife

137

in reality for years—some psychic block—I always wanted an heir, you know—but she, well—

Oh, he could convince a board of officers. Especially with every man-jack of them thinking guiltily about their own Japanese mistresses. Buckley sucked at the bottle, grinned wetly with his bruised mouth. Beth wouldn't be so damned serene in a straitjacket.

Carrying his pillowcase and bottle, belly bulging over loud-striped shorts, shuffling along in the Japanese slippers he liked, Colonel Buckley went back into the living room, feeling much better already. Until he made out the men standing just inside the entrance.

"Hioshi?" he called thickly. "Damn you—I told you to stay out of here—get out, you leering Japanese swine!"

One man moved forward. Buckley frowned, blinking at him.

"Your butler isn't here, colonel," the man said. "Neither is your driver."

"What the hell—"

The man came out of the shadows into light. "Kojima is my name, colonel—Lieutenant John Kojima, Counter-Intelligence. My credentials."

Buckley swallowed, forced a ragged smile. "Ahh—the—the incident here tonight? Nothing for the CIC, lieutenant, I assure you. A little too much to drink—you understand—"

Stonily, Kojima waited until the colonel's hearty, man-to-man talk ran down of its own accord. Buckley drew himself up, remembered that it's impossible to look dignified in underwear, remembered that he held a bottle—and a pillowcase. The pillowcase!

"You'll excuse me, lieutenant. I—I was tidying up. Be with you in a minute. Then I'm sure we can iron this out—"

"Stay put," Kojima said. "Put down that bottle and sack—easy."

138

Buckley tried to bluster. "Watch yourself—*lieutenant*. You're talking to a superior officer, a—"

"I'm talking to a *suspect*," Kojima snapped. "Now drop that stuff and back off—or do you want me to take them away from you? I hope so, colonel—you don't know how much I hope so."

Stunned, Buckley opened his hands. The open bottle thumped on the rug, trickled liquid into a dark puddle. The pillowcase mounded itself into a small heap. "Now look—"

"Okay," Kojima said over his shoulder. "You heard the suspect; your men can start looking over the house."

He stooped for the pillowcase. "The others are from the Japanese Secret Police, working with me. They have a warrant."

Buckley paled; his legs gave away, dropped him on the couch. "The S-Secret Police? W-why, I don't understand—I don't—"

Compact, slim as a dagger, Kojima stood over the colonel. "I'll let you know where you stand. We found your wife outside; she had some interesting things to tell both of us. You're in trouble up to your fat mouth, colonel. Right up to your fat mouth."

"My wife? B-Beth is mad, insane! She-she came in here with a gun—threatened my guests—"

"And what did the guy with her do? You're lucky he didn't break your back, when you told him about Sueko."

"What—what's she got to do with—"

Kojima cut him off with a chop of one hand in the air. "A hell of a lot, colonel—one hell of a lot. With your wife's testimony, these tape recorder reels of your business deals, and the rest we're going to find, the Army's got enough on you to stick you in Leavenworth until you're an old, old man."

Buckley's face felt numb, frozen. He tried to make sounds come out of a suddenly dry mouth, and failed. He could only stare.

Kojima went on, implacably. "But Mr. Hara is going to have a prior claim on you. I'm sure a sharp cookie like you is familiar with the Status of Forces Agreement? Boiled down, it says the Japanese can try you for a felony. Kidnapping, colonel, is a serious offense in Japan. So is murder. You'd better start praying that it's only *attempted* murder."

Relentlessly, savagely, Kojima hammered at the shuddering, frightened man squatting like a drunken Buddha on the couch. "Do you have any idea what it's like, in a Japanese prison? Not much food, colonel; one blanket for the winters. A club across the head if you don't move fast enough. I'm sure they can punish you much more effectively than we can. But when—and if—you ever get out, we're going to be waiting. Now get dressed."

Words boiled out of Buckley, tumbled over each other in their eagerness. "I'll help—I'll cooperate, anything you say. Just don't let *them* take me. I'm an officer—a colonel—I demand my rights. Listen—the girl is on a boat in the bay; Sueko is being held on the *Tatsu Temma*, a fishing junk about a mile out. Getty owns it; that's it—Captain Ward Getty of the Military Police. He made me do it; blackmail, threats—you understand—"

"Shut up," Johnny Kojima said tiredly, "Just shut the hell up. Get dressed, or they'll haul you down to the station like that."

Outside the window that faced on a darkened garden, one man nudged another. Silently, cautiously, they snaked away through the shrubbery, moving like detached shadows. One of them was squat and wide-shouldered. One limped.

They came erect behind the servant's quarters, flattened to the wall of the maid's rooms. Kai Watanabe was stiff, tense. "We wait here," he whispered.

Saburo shook his head. "No. You heard. Sueko is in danger. She will be killed."

Flat, hissing, Kai's voice struck at him. "*Baka . . .*

140

fool! The Secret Police are all around this house, in the streets, because of you clumsy idiots. Two only, and one a woman. You could not kill them."

Kai closed out Saburo's mumbled excuses. The ambush had been well planned, his gunmen mingling with the noisy celebrants, waiting for the big American to come out. Only blind men could have missed. He listened to sounds in the big house, to the ambulance clanging away in the street. The Yankees had a philosophy with more than a grain of truth in it: 'If you want something done right, do it yourself.' And as he thought about things, the situation was becoming perfect to handle alone. First, this bumbling idiot; then all the birds in one nest—Getty, Sueko, Saxon, all lines converging upon the *Tatsu Temma*.

The colonel was lost, but he knew nothing of Kai Watanabe. The others did. Now that Getty had been named, the fat MP would name others. Sueko knew too much. And Brad Saxon—he would pay with his life for the loss of the House of All Nations, standing ruined, empty and profitless; for the shattered drug store in Yokohama, for the Club Naha being placed Off Limits. And incidentally, for the death of Juji Fukuoka, an excellent and loyal Judo man. Something was owed, too, for the bodies even now being hauled away by the Secret Police. All accounts would be settled on board the Dragon Junk, everything neatly tied up.

Kai listened to a growing stillness, to Saburo's labored breathing beside him. Perhaps there might still be a way to balance the books. The big Yankee could be made to pay for all damages, furnish money for a quick recovery. If he was yet alive when Kai reached the *Tatsu Temma*, he could be forced to the ransom note. This time, it would stick. There were subtle tortures Kai had long been familiar with; he would use them.

Slowly, his hand slid into his coat, eased the long, slim dagger out of the sewn-in case that held it flat

141

along his ribs. Cars were driving away from the big house now, lights were snapping off. Only the remaining servants were talking, their words excited and fuzzed across the yard.

"Saburo," Kai said, and thrust the dagger in between his ribs.

He held the man as Saburo choked and writhed against the wall, twisting the knife handle, angling the keen blade up and across inside the warm body. An excellent stroke, he thought when Saburo stopped jerking; well placed. He lowered the body soundlessly to the ground. One threat wiped off the ledger. Now for the others.

Kai wasn't seen as he vaulted the garden wall and walked smoothly to a car parked on the dark side street. While others sought the Dragon Junk from the docks, going the long way around, Kai's waiting speedboat would whisk him there in minutes. His lips peeled back from teeth in a hungry smile.

CHAPTER XIX

Burning rubber, Brad slammed the big car around the corner, crumpled a fender against a stanchion, and leaped out before the wheels stopped spinning. He ran along the docks, found the "Omori" sign, and knew this was the place. Somewhere out on the dark waters that lapped the pier, Sueko was being held on a boat. If she wasn't already at the bottom of the bay, her hair floating like a thundercloud around her small, dead face while black things scuttled across the muck to feed upon her.

The thought shook him, pushed him along the pier in search of a boatman, a fisherman—anyone who would take him out to find the *Tatsu Temma*. And he thought about Beth Buckley, the selfless courage of one woman who had freed him to find another woman.

Stooped, conical straw hat hiding his face, the man lurched out of the gathering fog. Brad caught his arm, poured bastardized Japanese and GI English at the frightened figure, holding tightly so the man couldn't run. He was old, bent from years of hauling heavy nets, and he didn't understand.

Brad snatched out his wallet, thrust a handful of bills at him. *"Tatsu Temma—Tatsu Temma—"* repeating the name until the aged fisherman hissed and nodded, clinging desperately to the wad of thousand-Yen notes a madman had forced upon him.

"Hai," the fisherman said. *"Tatsu Temma—"* and pointed vaguely at the ocean.

143

"*Wakaru*—you know? Take me there. *Hayaku, hayaku* . . . hurry. More money—*takusan Yen*."

This, the old man understood. He hobbled quickly to the end of the dock, inched down a bamboo ladder with Brad breathing down his neck. His boat was small and leaky, with one ancient sweep. With frantic gestures, Brad made him know that all he had to do was point; Brad would man the sweep. The fisherman shrugged and pointed.

The flat-bottomed skiff had never leaped across the waters the way it was doing now. Brad prayed that the creaking oar would hold together as he threw his weight into it, leaned back for the return sweep with his back muscles straining. The fisherman chattered from the bow, signalled to the left. Brad cut down the length of the strokes, dipped the blade in shorter arcs, swung the prow to port.

A foghorn bellowed; an invisible gull fluttered cursing out of the water. Fog curled past them; the boat nosed into a deepening swell, rocked and threw salt spray over its back like some live sea creature. Brad worked the sweep, chopped it into the water, shoulders heaving, forearms corded and knotted, big hands keeping a death grip on the worn handle.

"*Sokuryoku!*" the old man called back. "Slowly . . . *Tatsu Temma massugu ni* . . . straight ahead!"

Brad turned away from the long oar, peered into the fog-shrouded darkness, and saw the angular shape of a junk looming close. Fearfully, the old man darted past him to the stern, fought the sweep to bring the skiff about in a half-circle before it crashed into the black bulk of the Dragon Junk.

In ringing Japanese, a loud voice damned the boat owner who'd leap out of the fog that way. Another joined in; the old man screamed back at them. Brad jumped for the side of the boat, grunted as his ribs slammed into damp wood, and hooked his hands on a slick railing.

144

He had one knee over the rail when a light splashed brightness in his face.

"Yankee! *Korosu* . . . kill!"

Wooden soles of *geta* slapped the deck, blending with the rapid scuff of straw sandals. Men yelled throatily, drunkenly. Brad caught Getty's name as a flung fist crashed against the side of his head. He shook it off, threw his other leg over the rail, and rolled into a flying block.

A gun crashed as men went down like bowling pins. A flung club clattered into the mast. Brad reached out, hauled a man to him kicking and screaming. A knee drove into his stomach, low and agonizing. Brad grunted, hammered a fist at a blurred face. Something exploded at the back of his head, hurled him face down and skidding across the damp planking.

Dazed, he came to his knees, fumbled for a grip on anything, found a cold length of chain and pulled himself up. The gun went off again, slapped a bullet past his ear. Men yelled; the junk rocked. Brad shook his head, cleared it in time to lift the chain and whirl it. It struck like a giant steel snake, rattling big, crushing links into the plunging forms around him. The yells turned to screams.

One man clutched the bloody ruin of his face and reeled backward to the rail. The cold waters of the bay cut off his moans. The chain sang through light-splashed fog, bit into meat and snapped bones. A pistol skidded across the deck as another man doubled over the raging lash that had almost cut him in half, that had three grave-cold links buried deep into his shattered ribs. Brad yanked at the chain, jerked the gurgling man across the planks, ducked away from the knife-tipped lunge of a spitting Japanese.

He back-handed the head as it flashed in at him, ricocheted it off the rail and snapped his foot out in a timed kick as its distorted features bounced back. There was the sound of a melon dropped upon concrete. Brad sucked for air, roaring, springing like a

145

huge jungle cat at the only man he saw on his feet. Squealing, the Japanese leaped over the side, legs churning, arms flailing before he hit the water. Brad stood alone on the deck of the Dragon Junk.

The shriek came keening up from the hatchway amidships, full of pain and hate. A woman in agony, the sound torn from a straining throat. Sueko!

He threw himself at a sliver of yellow light, tore at the hatch cover and hurled it into the night. Brad leaped feet-first into the cabin below, landed on piled rugs with a spine-shaking thump, and whipped around to stare at the far end of the hold.

Gleaming nakedly and stretched painfully taut like an "X" of lovely flesh, Sueko hung between iron ringbolts. There was a fleck of blood on each of her daintily moulded breasts. A man caught up in the insane folds of a nightmare, Brad started for her.

Getty stepped out from behind the bar and aimed a .38 at Brad's middle. There was a sickly shine of sweat on his jowls; his flat eyes glittered from their blueshadow pouches. His fat hand held the bulldog pistol very steady.

"You had to keep pushin'," Getty said. "You had to keep comin', crowding me, crowding the colonel. So you found the wench."

Brad held himself carefully still, lifting only his eyes to look beyond the hairy nakedness of the man to find the girl's face. "Sueko."

Her mouth was uncurling roses. "Brad—"

Getty motioned abruptly with the .38. "Tender; very touching. Now tell her goodbye."

Brad stared at the man, measured the distance between them. "You'd better be good with that thing, Getty—you'd better be damned good."

The captain didn't answer. Smirking, his finger tightened on the trigger.

"Don't you want to know how I found you—how I knew where this boat was?"

Indecision flickered across Getty's face, darkened his eyes. The gun didn't waver.

"You're through," Brad said hurriedly. "All through. Buckley blew the whistle on you, told me where to find you. The CIC's got him by now."

The .38 jerked. Brad held his breath.

"Stalling," Getty said. "You're stalling."

"Kojima—Lieutenant Johnny Kojima. How would I know him?"

Getty ran his tongue over his lips. "That ain't enough."

"You damned fool. You think Colonel Buckley is going to take the rap alone? And Watanabe—how about Kai Watanabe?

"No more than the CIC does—and a guy named Hara in the Japanese Secret Police. They've got you tied in all around, Getty. The works. But they can't pin a murder charge on you. You don't want to hang, Getty."

The captain's thick mouth firmed. "No," he grunted, "and I don't want to spend the rest of my life behind bars, either. You came bustin' in here by yourself, Saxon. If the rest of 'em knew, why the hell ain't they with you?"

"Getty—"

The pistol pushed out. "Shut up. I can dump both of you in the bay, take the junk over across the harbor and sink her. I got money, Saxon—a hell of a lot of money, and it ain't all Stateside. Some of it's in Hong Kong."

His eyes glinted. "Yeah—that's the answer. You brought this on yourself, hero."

Brad tensed. "Hit me right, Getty—stop me with the first one, or I'll stick that gun down your throat."

"Hero," Getty grunted.

Sueko screamed behind him.

Something jarred the bulkhead of the *Tatsu Temma,* heeled the junk momentarily, canting her deck in unison with the noise of wood scraping wood. Involuntarily, Getty's eyes flicked toward the sound. For just a split second. It was enough.

A raging blur, Brad was at Getty. The .38 slammed, seared flame and the bite of a slug across Brad's left shoulder. Savagely, he chopped down with his right fist. The pistol exploded again when it bounced off the deck. Getty staggered back to the bulkhead, sweaty shoulders thumping against it.

Brad stepped over the smoking pistol, his scarred face chill and deadly. "I told you, Getty. I told you to make your first try good."

Getty scuttled desperately for the ladder, naked haunches spasming. Brad kicked him in the spine, drove his head into the ladder. Like an obscenely hairy balloon, Getty collapsed, slid down the steps to the deck.

Brad ran to Sueko, lifted himself to hook his fingers into the ringbolts and rip them from the ancient wood. The girl draped over his shoulder as he twisted the ones that held her ankles, pulled them shrieking metallically from the half-rotted flooring. Gently, he lifted her nude body and carried it to the heaped piles of brocade cushions.

He saw the whip, its braided lash sticky. He saw the cuts on Sueko's tender breasts. He placed her on the pillows and turned around.

Getty was stirring, struggling up to his knees with both trembling hands pawing at the ladder. Brad scooped the gun off the deck, a red haze blotting out everything but the fat worm before him. He worked his weakening left hand into Getty's hair, hammered a knee into the man's womanish breasts to quieten him.

Getty sobbed, beat ineffectually at Brad with damp hands. Brad twisted, brought the face tilting up. Getty's mouth gaped wide and wet. Brad brought the gun around, and Getty's eyes bulged as he saw what Brad was going to do with it. He screamed once, then locked his teeth and clawed at the gun, at the corded forearm holding him helpless.

Brad shoved the gun muzzle against the thick lips, split them, rolled the weight of his shoulder behind his arm and forced the snub barrel into the teeth. They snapped. Getty tried to scream again, but his mouth was full of oiled metal, crammed with agony and filling rapidly with thick, gushing blood as the gunsight tore the back of his throat. Getty choked. He fought madly to wrench away, to disgorge the hard pain, to breathe around the pressure and through the hot liquid.

It was no good. A great weight forced the gun deeper, grating on the stumps of splintered teeth, forced it down and back while the thunder grew in his ears. From very far away, Getty could hear a faint, echoing voice repeating no-no-no . . .

"No, Brad—No!" Sueko pulled at his arm with all her strength, tugged at him until his stony face turned to her and the granite slowly faded out of it.

"You mustn't kill him," she said. "No, no. Leave him, Brad—let the police take him, the MPs."

The red curtain lifted itself. Her eyes were sleek, dark almonds, so intent, tear-dampened around their lashes. Sueko. The small, perfect body fitted into his arms. Her lips were sweet, sorrow-sweet and satiny. Sueko. He said her name aloud, holding her trimness to his body.

"Sueko—"

The man at their feet was forgotten. Retching, blinded by agony, Getty lay with one jowl soaked in a pool of blood, the stained pistol inches away from his wrecked mouth. His bare feet jerked in the running motions that a wounded rabbit makes. Another foot—short and wide and shining in expensive English leather—nudged a polished toe against the wet .38 and spun it across the cabin, out of reach.

"You should have kept the pistol," Kai Watanabe said.

Brad thrust Sueko behind him protectively as he turned.

Kai smiled. His eyes didn't. The dagger gleamed in his hand, held low with a thumb along its blade. "I'm not as slow as Captain Getty."

"Back out," Brad said. "Nobody takes this girl away now. Nobody."

Kai's oily smile expanded. "Of course not. But you and I have some unfinished business." His voice hardened. "Don't try it! That left arm is wounded, I see—hanging limp. The odds are against you, Saxon-*san*."

"I'll tell you as I told Getty," Brad said. "You're through, Watanabe. The Secret Police know who you are; they'll run you down. And the CIC have you pegged, too."

Kai was watchful as a mongoose before a coiled cobra, the knife poised, his weight balanced on both feet, ready to move. "Not quite through," he said. "The ransom, remember? You'll write the letter this time, Saxon-*san*. Back away, now—very slowly and carefully."

Brad's left arm throbbed; he felt the bullet nick oozing blood. Kai was right; the arm was useless—or almost so. He needed a few minutes; Kai wanted a ransom note. All right, he'd get it. Brad backed away, making Sueko move behind him.

Getty moaned on the deck. Still smiling, Kai stooped quickly and slashed the dagger across Getty's exposed throat, his hand skipping ahead of the red geyser. Straightening, Kai said gently: "So you will realize that I'm serious, Saxon-*san*."

Sueko hid her face in her hands. Brad's mouth thinned. "You didn't have to do that."

"Oh, but I did. Captain Getty was a problem for me. Now the problem is solved." Kai's voice snapped then: "To the table! Write the letter!"

150

Brad hesitated. "And if not—"

"I will put this dagger into you so you die slowly. Then I will use it on Sueko. Her navel, perhaps—turning the blade gently. Or lower down—"

"Okay," Brad said. "Okay, the letter."

But he knew Kai Watanabe had no thought of allowing Sueko and himself to leave the boat alive. The squat, grinning killer probably had it all planned out —two quick slashes, more bodies over the side, a run to some deserted boat slip. With a letter that would sooner or later bring him the money he needed to stay hidden.

"Then it was your boat that bumped this one?" he asked. "It stopped Getty from pulling the trigger."

"I'm happy for both of us," Kai said. "You waste time. Quickly; there's a pen and paper beside the cigar box."

Brad watched the man. Kai was in a hurry, more worried than he showed, and a little more sure of his knife work than he should be. Fleetingly, Brad wondered if Kai were a Judo expert like the man who'd almost gotten him in Beth Buckley's house.

"Is Hara right behind you? That why you're so jumpy?"

Kai stopped smiling. The knife glinted in short, weaving arcs before him. "So you realize that I must kill you both? Very well. If you wish to save the girl from needless pain, you'll write the letter quickly. I will promise you that she will die swiftly."

"You *promise*," Brad spat. "You said something when you came in, buster. You said I should have kept Getty's pistol. *You* should have kept it."

Kai saw Brad fall into a crouch, and dropped back hissing through his teeth. The dagger flashed back and forth across Kai's body with the hypnotic eagerness of a swaying rattlesnake. Step by step, left arm dangling, right arm crooked wide, Brad moved in, chin tucked into his broad chest, eyes watching the knife through lowered and twisted eyebrows.

Kai moved well, light on his feet with the trained alertness of the Judo man, poised and ready. There was one chance. Brad had to take that blade—not in his hand, but into his body. Kai wouldn't be expecting that; no knife man would. Kai would expect his victim to try a quick lunge, a spin to avoid the striking blade. It wouldn't be that way. Brad had to get close, get his one good hand on the chunky little killer. And he had to hope that the knife missed a vital spot.

Brad leaped forward, straight in. In swift reflex, Kai stabbed out and up. Cold and sharp, the blade lanced into Brad's muscled stomach like the deft scalpel of a surgeon. He felt it cut deep, as his momentum carried him crashing into Kai, felt the ice-slick blade grate along the curve of a rib.

But his chest thrust into Kai, swept him back and into the bulkhead. His hooked right arm closed in, looped around the Japanese's torso. He had him. No matter what the knife blade was doing to Brad's guts, he had Kai Watanabe just where he wanted him.

Brad lowered his head, jammed it against Kai's shouting face, rubbed it hard into the mouth and chin, pinning the sinuous man solidly. Then he winced from a chop across the back of his neck, lifted a knee to slam it into Kai's groin. The other knee; changing over, one after another, pistoning. Driving, battering at the soft underbelly, ripping and tearing with implacable force into Kai's jerking body.

Kai got a thumb into Brad's eye. Brad turned his chin and locked his teeth into the base of the thumb until they grated on bone. Another knee pounding, another, and suddenly Brad was conscious that he was working on a body that had turned to jelly. He pulled back his head, staggered away from Kai so the man could slip to the deck.

Brad couldn't see very well; just enough to make out the hilt of the dagger angling out of his rib cage.

He touched it with curious fingers. Sueko ran sobbing to him, her eyes horrified.

"Brad—oh Brad—"

Somehow, the tide in the bay was surging through his ears with each gentle roll of the flooring beneath his feet. His bad knee sagged. Brad braced a hand against a post. "I'm okay—I'm okay—" but there was a great weakness in him.

And they weren't going to let him rest. Feet dropped down the ladder, pattered toward them. Brad knuckled his eyes, pushed away from the post, swept the girl behind him again. Dark little men with mouths open, yelling, coming at him. Wearily, he reached out at them and they skipped away, shouting, waving their hands.

The deck felt soft against his cheekbone when he fell.

CHAPTER XX

The first time he opened his eyes, there was only a woman in the room, crisp in white starchy things; a face like scrubbed stone. The Forty-Niner trainer had a face like that—only seamed and cracked with age; and generally unscrubbed. Brad wondered what a woman was doing in the dressing room, and went back to sleep.

Next time, it was with late afternoon sunlight slanting across his bed, with a stiffness in his left side and tape over his left shoulder. And there were two women. They didn't have faces like stone.

Sueko—joy stamped on her quivering mouth, an uncertain glory balanced hopefully in her eyes.

Beth—sad flower, a maturing radiance lighting her from within.

"Hey," Brad said.

Tiny and trim, Sueko leaned over him, touched his hand. "I'll be back."

"Don't go far," he said. "It might hurt if I run."

"Not far," she murmured, and left him with Beth Buckley.

Beth's ripe lips parted. "Should you be sitting up like that?"

"Beth—that was a brave thing you did for me. I tried to get back; the bunch with guns—"

Her smile was tremulous. "Mr. Hara's men. You almost ran them down. I—I don't think I was very brave. I just—wanted to do something to help. For once. I wanted something for somebody else. Does that sound silly?"

"No," he said. "Beth, I—"

"Hush now. Everything's finished. Jerry is where he belongs—in prison. Captain Getty will be, too—if he ever gets out of his straitjacket. He sits and cries that he's choking. Kai Watanabe died yesterday. Mr. Hara found a notebook in his pocket, with enough information to smash the organization. You'd better lie down."

"I feel fine," Brad said. "Except for—"

"Me?" Beth smiled faintly. "Don't be sorry for me, Brad. And don't let Sueko be. I'll soon be a free woman—freer than I've ever been. I—I can start over. If I keep looking, somewhere, some time, I'll find another—another guy as ugly—and as sweet. Take care of her, Brad. She's a—a wonderful girl."

"I know another one," he said.

"Well enough to—to kiss her goodbye?"

His side twinged as he leaned forward. Beth's lips were cool, tasting vaguely of salt, of secret regrets. Only a feather-touch, and they were gone. He watched her walk proudly away—tall, firm, her back erect, chin held high. Brad hoped that the guy she found would realize how lucky he was.

All finished, she had said. Watanabe, Getty, Buckley—all finished. Shrewd little Hara was probably happy. Johnny Kajima, too. That tied it up all around. Except for Sueko. What did Hara and his outfit have in mind for her? There was still the question of her involvement with Watanabe. Brad had just swung his legs over the side of the bed when the door opened.

The Japanese doctor was brisk, horrified when he saw Brad's feet on the floor. "Please—back to bed."

The nurse behind him moved forward to help, rustling, frowning. "Mr. Saxon—the stitches—"

Brad wasn't interested. Framed in the doorway, Sueko waited, a picture all the artists in the world

155

couldn't paint. A bare, sterile hospital room was no place for the things he had to say to her. Brad stood up. For just a second, his head spun, and when he took a deep breath, his side reminded him of a quick sharp dagger.

"Where are my clothes?"

"Mr. Saxon—as your doctor I must insist—"

Brad looked down at his bare legs. The hospital gown was probably the biggest they could find, but about three sizes too short. It looked like one of those shortie nightgowns curvy models wore. He wasn't built for it. His backside was cool, because they'd only been able to tie the top string—the one around his neck.

"My clothes," he repeated.

"Hospital rules—you've been seriously wounded—"

"Okay," Brad said, "so I go like this. Anybody faints in the halls, send the bill to me—Nomura Hotel."

Open-mouthed, Sueko skipped along beside him because he held her by the elbow. Brad's big feet slapped the cold marble of the floors, leaving a trail of giggling nurses and shocked attendants behind them. For a moment, at the entrance, he thought he'd pushed it too far, that he was going to plop his naked stern on the steps. But he shook off the feeling. The taxi driver took one startled look at him and was afraid not to haul them away.

"Don't say anything," Brad said, the leather seat chill against where his hip pockets ought to be. "I'll lay it all out for you first. Then you can tell me to go to hell or forgive me. I was wrong, Sueko—a thick-headed damned fool for ever leaving you. I thought a lot of things were more important—college, preparing for the job my old man wanted to see me in—stupid things like that."

Her eyes were tender. "Brad—"

"Let me finish. It took me nine lonely years, eating my heart out every day of it, fumbling around for

156

a woman who could take your place. None of them could; none of them ever could. I kept telling myself that you were just another girl—that if you hadn't played Madame Butterfly for me, it would have been some other guy—any other guy. And I told myself that you were doing okay with hundreds of GIs, that I was nothing special to you—only the first."

Eyes brimming, Sueko cupped one small hand on his arm. Brad stared out of the taxi window, afraid to look at her. He said, "Then it was money; I had to get enough of it. But when I did, it only meant that I could come back to you. Sueko—if you can accept it from an idiot, I'm sorry. I love you. I want you to marry me. Now—if you want to tell me to go jump in the bay, you've sure as hell got the right to."

The taxi jolted to a stop. "Nomura Hotel," the driver said. "How you pay—no pockets?"

Sueko opened her purse, passed the man a bill.

"Are—are you coming in?" Brad asked.

Eyes lowered, a faint spray of roses staining her cheeks, Sueko said: "I will come in."

At the desk, a clerk impeccable in bowtie and white jacket swallowed hard and stared before turning to walk determinedly to the office. The elevator boy grinned behind his hand. Sueko found something to watch on the floor.

In an upper hall, a man heard the elevator doors clang shut and got hurriedly off the chair he'd been warming. Brad leaned out, touched the knob. The door swung back. He half-turned, stooped without flinching, and looped a crooked elbow behind Sueko's nyloned knees. He lifted her, stood up.

"In my country," he said, "it's customary to carry the bride into the room. But if you'd rather wait until I can get the marriage license and the minister—"

"B-Brad—darling—you are hurt—you are too weak to—to do—"

"To do what I have in mind?" He grinned, stepped

into the room and heeled the door closed behind them. "When I'm *that* weak, baby, I'll be *dead.*"

She stood beside the bed, oblique eyes direct, deep. "In my country," she said, "a new wife takes off her husband's shoes. You have no shoes—but if you bend over, I can reach the string around your neck."

He bent. And saw the patchwork bandage across his ribs and belly, felt the pull of tape on his shoulder as the gown fell away. Then he saw her unbuttoning her blouse, saw the skirt whisk away from perfectly turned legs that gleamed golden in the light.

Sueko wore nothing beneath her outer clothing, because she didn't need anything. Ivory cones of her breasts lifted proud coral caps to him; the miniature flowers of her thighs beckoned, the breathtaking sweep of downy stomach and exquisitely flared hips.

They came together tenderly, gently seeking, but with a knowing of each other, a fitting and blending that the years that had stood between them had not been able to erase. She was familiar, and yet she was new, as she would always be to him. Leg-locked, metronoming in a sweetly swiftening staccato, they meshed in a dampwarm melody that sang through every fiber of their bodies, that rose and fell with flesh and bone and taut muscle, that fingered trilling notes of ecstasy into long-unstirred depths and set them bubbling.

With the sighing of tensed strings, with the silvered explosion of trumpets and the ringing crash of cymbals, the music burst in starnotes that thundered in a mighty spasm of celestial rhythm, hurling them to a far, enchanted place. There was no one else in the world. There would never be anyone but shadow-people. Brad had found his woman again, and with her, found himself.

Outside, in the hall, Lieutenant Johnnie Kojima looked thoughtfully at the closed door of the room. Then he scratched his chin, shrugged and went back to sit in the chair on the other side of the elevator.

A few minutes later, the elevator shaft rumbled, yawned open its doors and let another man out. Kojima was quicker this time, and was at the man's side before he'd taken four steps.

"Mr. Hara."

The little man blinked through his glasses. "You were right, although even the doctors believed he would not walk for another week. The girl is with him?"

Kojima grinned. "Naturally."

Mr. Hara nodded. "Then I must hurry. There are those who wish to see her punished for her part in the betrayal—and not all of these people are my countrymen."

"I know," Kojima said, "There are a couple of jerks in the Ambassador's office—but he can get her out of the country until the uproar dies down. She was forced into helping Watanabe, after all."

"Yes," Mr. Hara said. "But Tokyo is a bad place for them at the moment. Therefore, I must give them the visas I carry—and the airplane tickets to Hong Kong. The Secret Police will be diligently looking for Miss Kamiya—everywhere but the airport. The third room, I believe?"

"Wait. I wouldn't go in there. Not now. I wouldn't even knock on the door."

Mr. Hara frowned. "But—time is important. There is a plane leaving in one hour, and—"

Kojima cut in. "Mr. Hara, Brad Saxon traveled thousands of miles. He wrecked a bar, a hotel, a boat, men I haven't even got counted yet—and half the communist spy network in Japan. He fought his way through all this to get to a girl—the girl in there with him now. He likes you, Mr. Hara. But just what the hell do you think a man like that would do if you disturbed him when he's alone with her for the first time? Think about it, Mr. Hara. Then, if you want to go bang on his door—go ahead. But give me a head start. I'd like to be on the other side of town."

159

Mr. Hara considered. "It is written that impatience is a failing, and one that the Japanese must avoid. There is another chair down the hall?"

Kojima grinned. "Yeah. Clever people, we Orientals, eh?"